Satisfaction ran thro ~~surveyed the woman~~ **Alexa Harcourt in evening attire was all that he wanted her to be.**

Superbe.

As she stood before him in the rich, lustrous beauty she was finally revealing to him, anticipation speared within him for what he knew would be the delights of the evening ahead.

Not that she gave any sign yet of realizing that was to happen. She was, he knew, quite unconscious of what—with absolute inevitability—lay ahead. It would, of course, make seducing her even more *piquant*—even more enticing!

And now, the evening was about to begin.

"Shall we?" he invited.

She walked with superb grace, he noted, although there was the very slightest tension in her shoulders. As if she were not entirely at ease.

Yes, she was indeed well worth his time and attention. Pleased with his choice, Guy relaxed fully into the leather seats and appreciatively continued his surveillance. To his pleasure, the evening stretched ahead of him.

And the night—ah, the night would be exceptional....

All about the author...
Julia James

JULIA JAMES lives in England with her family. Harlequin® novels were the first "grown-up" books Julia read as a teenager (alongside Georgette Heyer and Daphne du Maurier), and she's been reading them ever since.

Julia adores the English countryside (and the Celtic countryside!) in all its seasons, and is fascinated by all things historical, from castles to cottages. She also has a special love for the Mediterranean (the most perfect landscape after England!). She considers both ideal settings for romance stories! Since becoming a romance writer, she has, she says, had the great good fortune to start discovering the Caribbean, as well, and is happy to report that those magical, beautiful islands are also ideal settings for romance stories! "One of the best things about writing romance is that it gives you a great excuse to take holidays in fabulous places!" says Julia. "All in the name of research, of course!"

Her first stab at novel writing was Regency romances. "But alas, no one wanted to publish them!" she says. She put her writing aside until her family commitments were clear, and then renewed her love affair with contemporary romances. "My writing partner and I made a pact not to give up until we were published—and we both succeeded! Natasha Oakley writes for the Harlequin® Romance line, and we faithfully read each other's works in progress and give each other a lot of free advice and encouragement!"

In between writing, Julia enjoys walking, gardening, needlework and baking "extremely gooey chocolate cakes"—and trying to stay fit!

Julia James

FORBIDDEN OR
FOR BEDDING?

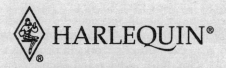

HARLEQUIN®

TORONTO • NEW YORK • LONDON
AMSTERDAM • PARIS • SYDNEY • HAMBURG
STOCKHOLM • ATHENS • TOKYO • MILAN • MADRID
PRAGUE • WARSAW • BUDAPEST • AUCKLAND

Recycling programs
for this product may
not exist in your area.

ISBN-13: 978-0-373-12960-7

FORBIDDEN OR FOR BEDDING?

First North American Publication 2010.

Copyright © 2010 by Julia James

FORBIDDEN OR
FOR BEDDING?

PROLOGUE

MILD autumnal sunshine was filtering through the kitchen window of Alexa's flat on the borders of Notting Hill, illuminating the pinewood table set for breakfast for two. The simple but elegant pottery creamware and silver-plated cutlery had been acquired painstakingly and piecemeal from antiques shops. Bright flowers adorned the table in a glass vase, and the aroma of freshly made ground coffee hung in the air.

So did a tension that Alexa would have had to be a block of stone not to feel.

She had had no inkling of it until this moment. Until this moment her mood had been languid—sensual, even—for making love upon waking was something that never failed to leave her with a sense of rich well-being that lasted all the day long—even on days like this when, unlike the previous night, she would go to bed alone.

But she was used to that by now. Used to going from a night of sensual overload that left her dazed, swept to shores she had once known nothing of but to which now she was a familiar, oh, so familiar traveler, to abstinence. But as she stood by the table, coffee pot in hand, her slender body concealed by nothing but a pale green silk peignoir, her long, still slightly tousled hair rippling down her back, she felt her throat give a little catch, as though her body—more than her body—remembered with absolute clarity that sense of wonder, almost disbelief, that would sweep her away on a tsunami of emotion.

Not that she ever revealed that emotion. Only the passion with which it was expressed. The emotion itself could never be acknowledged.

For a moment—an endless, empty moment—bleakness showed in her eyes. Then it was gone. She had accepted, had *had* to accept, that all she could have was what she had now. These brief, precious times when she would burn with an intensity that transformed her life, which carried her through the intervening days and nights of celibacy until her phone would ring and everything else became secondary, inconsequential, irrelevant. Her friends, her work, her whole life—all put aside.

And then for one night, perhaps two, perhaps—so rarely—more, when the call summoned her to a private airfield and whisked her away within an hour of the summons to some continental city or—even more rarely, even more blissfully—to some Italian villa, some Alpine ski lodge, some Monagasque penthouse, she would give herself entirely to the moment. However brief, however fleeting.

Was she rash, foolish, intemperate to be so? Of course she was! She knew it—knew it with every last ounce of sense within her. Good sense. Sense that tempered, as it must—should—that volatility of emotion which was the other half of her, that intensity of emotion that fuelled not just her life but her art. Sense that kept her outward persona cool, composed—controlled.

That was what others saw. The persona she deliberately projected. Few of her friends, especially those in the heady and passionate world of art, realised that her outward appearance of dispassionate calm in fact concealed an inner intensity of emotion—emotion that she channelled only into the art that she painted for herself, not for her profession. Others saw a tranquil beauty—a pale, silken-haired English rose—but few recognised the flame that burnt deep, deep within her.

Raised by parents who had led ordered, intellectual lives, Alexa knew that they had been taken aback to discover their only child was as artistically talented as soon became evident during her schooldays. They had not opposed her choice of subject—far from it—but Alexa had always recognised that they found it faintly astonishing that their daughter should have taken so to art which, to their sedate minds, was associated with stormy passions, extreme emotions and, worst of all, a tendency to lead disordered and messy lives.

Was that why—almost as a favour to her parents, perhaps—she had schooled herself to be as unlike a temperamental artist as she could? Why she enjoyed a tranquil, ordered existence, keeping her outward life calm and temperate and restraining her emotionality to her work? Yet she knew that it also came naturally to her to be reserved, dispassionate, self-contained, and once she had graduated from art school she ran her professional life as smoothly as her personal life.

As for men… Drawn by her pale beauty, they had come and gone—but mostly gone, for they had not, Alexa had known, been special to her. So she reserved herself on that score as well, enjoying the company of a select few boyfriends, with whom she mostly enjoyed going to the theatre, to concerts, to art exhibitions. Emotionally, though, she was untouched, and physically none had ever set her afire to explore the sensual promise of the body. No one had succeeded in lighting that flame hidden so deep within her.

No one but the man who stood there now, paused in the

doorway, a man who, every time her eyes rested on him, made the breath catch in her throat, her pulse quicken. Every time.

As it did now.

He stood there, dominating the physical space just as he dominated her mental space, six foot of lean masculinity sheathed in an immaculately hand-made pale grey suit, with an effortless elegance about him that only served to emphasise his maleness while indicating his continental heritage. Guy de Rochement would never be taken for an Englishman, yet his French surname was only a fraction of the complex pan-European inheritance that had made the banking house of Rochement-Lorenz a byword for wealth, prestige and power.

Now, those extraordinary long-lashed eyes that could melt Alexa into quivering jelly by a single glance were resting on her. She felt, as she always did, their power, but now, for the first time, she also felt, deep within her, something different—the tension that seemed to set the air between them vibrating with a fine disturbance of the equilibrium.

She paused, waited, the coffee pot that she had been holding as he'd walked into the sunlit kitchen still in her hand. Suddenly the kitchen seemed less bright, less warmed by the sunshine. Time stretched between them, tangible, tense—it seemed to last for ever, and yet it was only the beat of a single heart.

Then he spoke.

'I have something to tell you.' Guy's accent in English was almost perfect, but not quite, still holding a faint sussuration of French, Italian, German—any of the half-dozen languages he'd grown up speaking amongst his polyglot relatives. His voice was clipped, and as she heard it Alexa felt the first tremor of emotion deep within her—an emotion she would have given the world not to feel. It was an emotion she would give no name to, would deny completely, because to admit it would be to open within her a door so dangerous it might destroy her. It was a door she must never open—no matter what Guy did, what he said.

Even when it was the words he was saying now. She heard the words, but they came from very far away, from a place she'd dreaded, feared. His clipped, reserved expression told her far more than the words themselves, though each syllable was like a scalpel slicing across her bare flesh.

'I'm getting married,' said Guy de Rochement.

Alexa was standing very still. Almost as if she were a statue, he thought irrelevantly—for his mind was doing strange things to him, despite the self-control he was ruthlessly exerting on himself right now. A statue by one of those absurd and over-inflated contemporary artists with no more talent than an ability to mock greatness, a woman in a kitchen holding a coffee pot as if it were a Greek urn. He, too, seemed frozen. Or at least his mind did. He had walked into the kitchen knowing what he had to say, and knowing the implications of it.

Those implications were clear. Unambiguous. Unavoidable.

Completely obvious to him.

A minute frown shadowed his eyes momentarily.

Were they as obvious to her, though?

He went on studying her for the space of another heartbeat as she stood there, perfectly motionless, as if frozen in time. Nothing seemed to register in those luminous, clear-sighted eyes that had so entranced him from the very first moment he had seen her. Eyes arrestingly beautiful, set in a face that even *his* high standards for female allure could not fault. Her beauty was completed by possession of a figure of slender perfection that had immediately, irrevocably captured his interest—an interest that he had pursued with all his customary ruthlessness when it came to such matters.

Some women, when he had shown an initial speculative interest, had sought to intrigue him further by playing pointless games—which, he assumed, they believed would entice him the more, encourage his pursuit or, even more presumptuously, serve as a means to exert control over him. But Alexa had, to his satisfaction, shown no such predilection for futile attempts to manipulate him. From the first she had shown no disingenuous reluctance, coyness or coquetry, and even when seduction had been accomplished, and he had begun his affair with her, she had recognised implicitly the terms under which it was to be conducted, and complied with them without demur.

Complied without demur with everything he wanted. Right from their very first night together…that unforgettable night…

In his mind, memory flickered like a flame in dry undergrowth. He sluiced it instantly. That fire must be put out—permanently. With all the discipline he habitually exerted he doused the flickering memory. This was not a time for memory—it was a time for clarity.

Brutal clarity if need be.

He needed to say it. Not just for her, but for himself as well. To make it crystal-clear…

She was standing immobile still, and something in her very stillness made the tension pull at him. Tension he did not want to feel.

Time to make things clear.

Cool and terse, the words fell into the space between them.

'I shan't be seeing you again, Alexa.'

For the space of another heartbeat time held still. An eternity of time in the briefest span. Then, like a film starting to play again, her body unfroze. With her customary graceful movements she lowered the coffee pot to its slate mat on the table and started to depress the plunger, letting the dark pungent liquid settle, then pouring it carefully out into one of the creamware cups. Gracefully she lifted the cup and saucer, proffering it to the man standing such a short space away from her.

Such an infinite distance now.

'Of course,' she answered. Her voice was serene, untroubled. '*C'est bien entendue*—that's the correct French, isn't it?' Her tone was conversational, unexceptional. 'Are you having coffee before you go?'

There was no emotion in her face as she spoke.

She would permit none.

In her hand, the coffee cup she was rock-steady. Not a tremor. She caught the scent of coffee coiling into the air, the molecules wafting upwards. Her eyes were resting on his face, limpid, untroubled. As if he had merely uttered a pleasantry of no consequence or significance.

He did not take the cup. His face remained closed, unreadable. But then she did not seek to read it. Sought only to hold the cup as steady as a rock, to hold her gaze as steady. It was as though a section of her brain had dissociated itself from the rest of her and was operating in a space all of its own.

For one last heartbeat she held the cup, then slowly—infinitely slowly—lowered it to the table. Her regard went back to him, still showing nothing in her eyes except politeness.

'I hope you will permit me to wish you every happiness in your forthcoming marriage,' she said, her voice as untroubled as her regard.

Smoothly, she moved towards the door, indicating thereby that she recognised he would take his leave now—coffee untouched, affair disposed of. She did not pause to see if he was following her, merely headed unhurriedly, gracefully, the silken length of her peignoir brushing against her bare legs, across the narrow entrance hall of her flat to the front door.

She heard rather than saw him follow her. She slid back the security bolts that were inevitable in London, even on a quiet, tree-lined road such as the one she lived on. She stepped back, holding open the door for him. He came forward, halted one moment, looked at her one moment. His face was still closed, unreadable.

Then... 'Thank you,' he said.

He might have been thanking her for her felicitations, but Alexa knew that he was not. Knew that he was thanking her for something he appreciated far more. Her acceptance.

His eyes still held hers. 'It has been good, *non*?'

Laconic to the last. She, too.

'Yes, it has.'

Briefly, like swansdown, she leant forward to brush with the lightest touch his cheek.

'I wish you well.'

Then she stood back.

'Goodbye, Guy,' she said.

For one last time her eyes held him. Then, with the merest nod of acknowledgement of her farewell, he walked out.

Out of her life.

She did not watch him go. Instead she shut the door. Slowly—very slowly. As if it weighed more than she could bear. Then slowly—very slowly—she leant back against it, staring expressionlessly across the hallway. There was no sound. Not even his footsteps descending the flight of steps.

Guy was gone. The affair was over.

Slowly—very slowly—her fingers curved into the palms of her hand.

Gouging deep.

Guy's car was waiting for him at the kerb. He'd phoned for it as he dressed, knowing that he would want it there for as soon as he'd told Alexa what he must. He had put it off for as long as it was possible. Until it was no longer possible to stay silent. As he walked down the stone steps from the front door of the terraced house of which Alexa's apartment occupied the top floor, his driver got out and came round to open the rear passenger door for him. He got in, barely acknowledging the gesture.

As he sank back into the soft leather seat his face remained expressionless.

Well, it was done. Alexa was out of his life. And she wouldn't be coming back.

Guy reached for the neatly folded copy of the *Financial Times* his driver had placed carefully beside him, and started to read.

There was no expression in his face. His eyes.

He would permit none.

Alexa was cleaning the bathroom. She should have been working, but she couldn't. She'd tried. She'd mixed colours, got herself ready, put up a brand new canvas, dipped her brush in the colours, lifted it to the canvas.

But nothing had happened. She'd hung, frozen, like an aborted computer program, unable to continue.

Jerkily she'd lowered the brush, eased off the surplus paint, and stuck it into turps. Then she'd blinked a few times, stared blankly ahead for a moment, before turning on her heel and walking out of her studio.

She'd walked into the kitchen and put the kettle on. But for some reason she hadn't been able to make a cup of tea. Or coffee. Or even run the tap for a glass of water. After a little while she'd gone into the bathroom.

She'd seen the bath could do with a clean, so she'd set to. That had seemed to work. Then she'd moved on to the basin, then the toilet pedestal, then the rest of the surfaces and walls. She rubbed hard, using elbow grease and a lot of household cleaner foaming on the sponge. It seemed to take a lot of cleaning, and she rubbed hard.

Harder and harder.

And as she rubbed and scrubbed her brain darted, like dragonflies scything across a pond with sharp, knifing movements. She wondered what the dragonflies in her brain were. Then she knew. Knew by their iridescent wings, their flash as they caught the light.

They were memories.

So many memories.

Stabbing and darting through her head. Memory after memory.

As sharp as knives.

Working backwards through time, taking her back, and back, and back.

CHAPTER ONE

Six months earlier....

'DARLING! You'll never *believe* who I've bagged for you!'

Imogen's voice came gushing down the line. Alexa, the receiver crooked under her ear, concentrated on catching the sheen on a petal that was proving tricky.

'Alexa? Are you there? Did you hear what I said? You'll never *believe* who—'

Alexa, who knew that Imogen could no more be halted in full flight than she herself could be dragged to the phone when she was painting by anyone other than her friend and business manager, interrupted.

'Who?' She knew Imogen was dying to be asked, so she could give the dramatic answer she was clearly bursting to give.

'He's absolutely *devastating*!' gushed Imogen. 'A million, zillion miles from *any* of the usual boring old suits.'

An extravagant sigh wafted down the line. Alexa wondered what Imogen was on about, then went back to working on the petal. She was dimly aware that Imogen was still in full flow, but didn't pay attention. Imogen loved to gush, and Alexa let her get on with it while she focussed on what was important at the moment.

Finally there was silence on the line.

'So?' came Imogen's prompt a moment later. 'Are you over the moon or what?'

Alexa frowned absently. 'What?'

An exasperated sign came into her ear. 'Darling, *do* pay attention! Put the paintbrush down and listen for two minutes. Even *you* are going to be impressed, I promise. *Guy de Rochement* phoned. Well,' Imogen temporised, 'not him personally, of course, but his London PA.' She paused. 'So, tell me you're impressed. Tell me—' her voice changed and adopted a husky timbre '—you're quivering all down your insides.'

Alexa, her paintbrush reduced to hovering over the canvas, intensified her slight frown.

'Quivering?' she echoed. 'What for?'

The exasperated sigh came again. 'Oh, really, Alexa, don't do that Little Miss Supercool with me! I'm not a bloke. And don't even *think* you'll be able to get away with it with Guy de Rochement. Not even *you* could do that. He'll have you swooning just like the rest of the female population.'

Alexa's brow furrowed. 'Am I supposed to know who this guy is?'

Imogen gave a trill of laughter. 'Darling—a pun! His name is Guy in English, but of course he's French—well, mostly—so it's pronounced with a long "*ee*". *Guy.*' She gave it a Gallic slant. 'Sounds *so* much sexier...' She gave another gusty sigh.

Alexa cut to the chase. She hadn't a clue what was going on, and didn't want any more of her time wasted.

'Imogen—who is he, why are you being so loopy about it, and what are you trying to tell me anyway?'

Imogen sounded more disbelieving than indignant. 'Don't tell me you've never heard of Guy de Rochement?

He's just all *over* the celeb mags! Only the posh ones, mind you! He's a triple-A-lister. Total class!'

'I don't read magazines like that,' replied Alexa. 'They're all rubbish.'

'Ooh, look at you. Hoity-toity!' shot back Imogen in mock admonition. 'Well, if you *did* sully your pure artistic soul with such guff you'd know who I was talking about—and why. Listen, even at *your* elevated heights I take it you've heard of Rochement-Lorenz?'

Recognition—not strong, but there all the same—was dredged into Alexa's forebrain. 'Mega-rich bankers all over the place and going way back into history?'

'That's them!' Imogen trilled. 'One of the *über*-dynasties across the Channel. Utterly rolling in it. Made pots of money in every country in Europe for the last two hundred years,' she reeled off. 'Just about financed the Industrial Revolution and bankrolled merchant fleets to every far-flung colony. They're so seriously into money and survival they even made it pretty much intact through the last century—both the World Wars, not to mention the Cold War—probably because they had family on every side going. And now they are riding higher than ever, despite the recession. And a *lot* of that is due to Guy de Rochement. He's the whiz-kid that's propelled the bank into the twenty-first century, and the whole vast clan just *slobbers* all over him because he's raking in the loot for them.

Her voice changed, adopting that husky tone again. 'Mind you, I'd take a punt it's the females in the family that do the most slobbering. Just like the females outside the family! I was practically salivating down the phone, and I was only speaking to his PA.'

Alexa cut to the chase again. Imogen was clearly bowled over by this *Guy* guy, whoever he was, and Alexa had certainly never heard of him.

'So what's the deal, Immie?' she asked.

'The *deal*, darling, is that he's interested in being painted by you!' cooed Imogen dramatically. 'And if he goes for it you'll be *made*, my sweet. No more dull old suits and cigars. You'll be able to take your pick of the A-listers—the really fab ones, up in the stratosphere. They're all as vain as peacocks, and they'll just *snap* you up. You'll be rolling in it!'

Alexa made a wry little face to herself. The whole portraiture kick had been Imogen's idea. When they'd both emerged from art college several years ago, her fellow student and friend had announced straight away that she was never going to be good enough to make anything out of art, and she was going to go into commercial management.

'And you'll be first on my books!' she'd informed Alexa gaily. 'I'll make you *pots* of money, see if I don't. No starving in garrets eating the acrylics for you, I promise!'

'I'm not really very interested in making money out of art,' Alexa had temporised.

'Yes, well,' Imogen had retorted, and Alexa knew there had been a touch of condemnation in her voice, 'not all of us can afford to be so high-minded.'

Then, immediately seeing the flash of pain in Alexa's eyes, she'd backtracked, hugging her friend.

'I'm sorry. My mouth sometimes… Forgive me?'

She'd been contrite, honestly so, and Alexa had nodded, hugging her back.

Imogen's family—large and rambling and open-hearted—had taken Alexa in, literally, during that first terrible term at art school, when Alexa's parents had been killed in a plane crash while coming back from holiday. Imogen and her family had got her through that nightmare time, giving her a refuge in her stricken grief, as well as helping her with all the practical fall-out from their deaths, which had included sorting out the best thing to do with what she had inherited. It was not vast riches by any means, but prudently invested it had provided Alexa with enough to buy a flat, pay her student fees and living expenses, and yield a small but sufficient income that meant she would have the luxury of not having to rely exclusively on her artistic career to live.

Even so, Imogen was dead set on turning her friend into a high-flyer in the art world.

'With your fantastic looks it's a dead cert!' she'd enthused.

'I thought it was whether I was any good or not,' Alexa had replied dryly.

'Yeah, right. That as well, OK. But come on—we know what makes the world go round, and good-looks definitely make it spin in your direction. You're a PR dream!'

But Alexa had been adamant. Something flash and showy and insubstantial in artistic terms was not what she was after. What it was exactly that she wanted, though, she was less sure. She enjoyed most media, most styles, was eclectic in her approach, and got completely absorbed in whatever she was doing. But then she got equally absorbed even if her next project was quite different. There was no clear artistic way forward for her.

Which was why, she knew, she had let Imogen have her head when she'd told her that she had a clear flair for portraiture—Alexa had painted Imogen's family to say thank-you for their kindness to her—and it would be a criminal shame to waste it. So when, out of her myriad contacts, Imogen had wangled a couple of commissions, Alexa had gone along with her friend's ambitions for her. And now, four years later, it had paid off handsomely—at least in financial terms.

It seemed she did indeed have a flair for portraiture,

for she had a generosity of spirit that enabled her to depict her sitters in ways that, whilst truthful, tended to show them in their best light. Considering that as Imogen moved her remorselessly up the fee scale her sitters became increasingly corpulent and middle-aged, that was no mean achievement. Yet, whatever her clients' unprepossessing exterior, Alexa found she enjoyed depicting the incisive intelligence, shrewdness, or sheer force of character that had got them where they were: to the upper reaches of the corporate ladder.

Which was why she was less than impressed at the prospect of having Guy de Rochement as a sitter. From what Imogen said he sounded no better than some kind of flash celebrity playboy, inheriting bucketloads and now merely swanning around the world making yet more. He would, she darkly surmised, be spoilt, conceited and full of himself—just because he was the scion of such a famous banking house.

Her thoughts darkened even more, recalling Imogen's drooling. And just because he happened to have a reputation for being sexy.

Alexa's mouth tightened. Rich, conceited and sexy. Great. He sounded like a royal pain in the proverbial.

Her opinion to that effect was only strengthened some days later when, Imogen having beavered away like crazy to set it up, Alexa's initial appointment with the fabled Guy de Rochemont was cancelled by phone at the last moment. The glacially indifferent PA's dismissive tone clearly told Alexa she was considered something little better than a minion—doubtless one of hundreds who waited on Guy de Rochemont's plutocratic convenience.

Automatically Alexa felt her hackles rise. So, when Imogen phoned her two hours later to ask breathlessly,

'Well, how did it go? Is he even more gorgeous in the flesh than in photos?' Alexa was icy.

'I have no idea. I was cancelled,' she said simply.

Imogen's reaction was immediately to temporise. 'Oh, darling, he's terribly, terribly busy—always flying off at the drop of a hat. And his PA's a cow anyway. So when have you rearranged for?'

'I neither know nor care,' was Alexa's terse reply.

Imogen wailed. 'Honestly, if you just *knew* how hard I'd worked to get you set up there! Hey-ho—I'll just have to suck up to the bovine PA and get another meeting sorted.'

She was back ten minutes later, cock-a-hoop. 'Jackpot! He's dining at Le Mireille tomorrow evening, and has agreed to meet you in the bar at seven forty-five beforehand.' She gave a trill of glee. 'Ooh, it's almost like a *date!*' she gushed. 'I wonder if he'll fall for your gorgeous English rose looks and be smitten in a *coup de foudre*? You must make sure you're looking absolutely *stunning!*'

Fortunately for her friend's blood pressure, Alexa made sure Imogen did not see her before she set off, with deep reluctance, to the ultra-fashionable watering hole the next evening. The moment she walked in she was extremely glad she had chosen to wear what she had. Every female there was in a number that screamed *Look at me!* By contrast, Alexa knew that her grey blouse and grey pencil skirt, with grey low-heeled shoes and matching bag, together with no make-up and hair repressed into a tight, businesslike bun, was designed to minimise her looks.

She gave her name—and that of the man she was due to meet—to the snooty-looking greeter inside the entrance. The woman's eyebrows lifted palpably as Alexa said Guy de Rochemont's name, and cast a sceptical glance over her unassuming appearance. Nevertheless she despatched a minion into the hallowed interior of the premises, where only the select few were permitted. The look of scepticism increased when the minion returned with a nod to indicate that, unlikely as it was, someone as dull looking as Alexa *was* of the slightest interest to such a man as Guy de Rochemont.

'It's a business appointment,' she said crisply, and then wished she hadn't—because why on earth did she care what a snooty greeter in a place like this thought one way or the other?

As she was led into the bar area—already crowded and filled with people noisily sounding off about themselves—her mouth tightened. This was not a place she'd have spent a single penny, even if she'd had the hundreds it required to dine here. It was showy, flash and superficial.

Was that what her prospective sitter was going to be like? Briefly she flicked her eyes around, looking for someone who might look like the way Imogen had so gushingly described him. There were certainly plenty of candidates. If egos had mass, the collective weight of self-regard in the room could have sunk the *Titanic*, Alexa thought waspishly. And doubtless Guy de Rochemont's ego would be a prime contributor. So which one was he? It could be any of them, Alexa acknowledged, for all the men looked sleek, rich, and unswervingly pleased with their own existence.

'M'sieu de Rochemont?'

The minion had halted, and the rest of what he said disappeared into French too fast for Alexa to follow. It was addressed to someone sitting at a low table. She could only see his back, shadowed by the minion's body. As the minion spoke to him he nodded briefly, and the minion beckoned her forward. She walked stiffly up to the unoccupied chair on the far side of the table, and sat down without waiting for either invitation or instruction.

'Good evening,' she said, her voice workmanlike, busying herself setting down her handbag. Then she lifted her eyes to the man seated opposite.

Could you hear the sound of a jaw dropping? she wondered, with some fragment of her brain that still functioned outside the complete fuzz that was suddenly her sole consciousness. Then another thought gelled. *Oh, hell, Imogen was right...*

Because, like it or not, whatever her scepticism had been, one thing was completely and irrefutably incontrovertible about Guy de Rochemont. He really was—well... She flailed about in her brain, trying to find words. Failing. Visual impressions raced through her mind—and more. Guy de Rochemont hit places that were far more than visual.

Visceral.

How—she scrambled for sense—how could a mere arrangement of features common to every human being vary so much in their impact? How was it that a combination of things that everyone else had—eyes, nose, mouth—could be so...so...

Her eyes skittered over him, taking in everything and anything—the sculpted face, the slant of his eyebrows, the thin blade of his nose, the finely shaped mouth, the edged line of his jaw, the sable hair that was perfectly framed around his head. She drank him in, unable to do anything else but succumb to the impact.

Dimly she was aware that he had half-risen at her appearance, but had sat back again as she had already sat down, and was now sitting with a kind of lean grace that—again—she could viscerally register without conscious assessment, one long leg crossed over the other and arms resting on the curving contour of the tub chair, relaxed and completely at ease with himself.

That's the pose, she felt herself think, feeling the familiar leap of conviction when the physical world arranged itself to perfection, ready for her to capture it to canvas.

Her eyes narrowed slightly, her brain still processing what her eyes were conveying to her. There was a rushing feeling going through her, a breathlessness. She was used to getting the buzz of pre-creation, but this was different. Far more intense...

Different.

She knew it was different—so different. She also knew she had never reacted in this way before in her life, but she pushed the knowledge to one side. She would deal with it later. Wonder about it later. Analyse it later. Right now... Right now all she wanted to do, all she *could* do, was simply let her eyes work over that extraordinary face, the incredible arrangement of features that just made her want to gaze and gaze and gaze at them.

Then, as if from far away, consciousness forced its way through. Awareness of what she was doing. Staring wordlessly at the man sitting opposite her.

Who was *letting* her gaze at him.

And even as the consciousness came through she felt, as if in slow motion, a wave of reaction. More than consciousness—self-consciousness. Her jaw tightened, and she stiffened, deliberately blinking to cut off her riveted perusal of him, regain some normality again. But it was hard. All she wanted to do, she knew, was to go right back to gazing at him, working her way over and over his features.

What colour are his eyes?

The question seared across her brain, and she realised she couldn't answer. It sent a thread of panic through her that she didn't know his eye colour yet. Her gaze pulled to get back to his face, to resume its study. She yanked it back. *No!* This was ridiculous, absurd. Embarrassing. She wasn't going to gaze at him gormlessly like a teenager! Or scrutinise him as if he were already sitting for her.

She straightened her spine, as if putting backbone into herself. Forced a polite smile to her mouth that was the right mix of social and business.

'I understand you are considering having your portrait painted?' she said. Her voice sounded, to her relief, crisp and businesslike.

For just a moment Guy de Rochemont did not answer her—almost as if he had not heard her speak. He continued to hold his pose, quite motionless, as if he were still under her scrutiny. He didn't seem to think it odd, she registered dimly, and then wondered just how long—or how—briefly—she'd been gazing at him. Perhaps it hadn't taken more than few seconds—she didn't know, couldn't tell.

Then, with the slightest indentation of his mouth, matching the socially polite smile Alexa had just given, he spoke.

'Yes,' he said. 'I've been persuaded to that ultimate vanity. The portrait will be a gift to my mother. She seems to consider it something she would like.' His voice was dry, and had a trace not just of an accent somewhere in his near perfect pronounciation, but of wry humour too. It also possessed a quality that, to Alexa's dismay, did very strange things to her. Things she busily pushed to one side. She gave a nod, and another polite smile.

'One thing, Mr de Rochemont, that I always warn clients about—should you wish to commission me, of course—is the amount of time that must be set aside for portraiture,' she began. 'Whilst I appreciate that calls on your time will be extensive, nevertheless—'

He held up a hand. It was, she saw, long, narrow, and

with manicured nails that gave the lie to a manicure being an effeminate practice.

'What would you like to drink, Ms Harcourt?'

Alexa stopped in mid-sentence, as if the question had taken her aback. 'Oh, nothing, thank you,' she said. 'I really don't have time for a drink, I'm afraid.'

Guy de Rochemont raised an eyebrow. Alexa felt her eyes go straight there. Felt the same rush of intensity that she had felt when she had first seen him. The simple movement on his part had changed the angles on his face, changed his expression, given him a look that was both questioning and amused.

'*Dommage,*' she heard him murmur. His eyes rested on her a moment.

They're green, she found herself thinking. *Green like deep water in a forest. Deep pools to drown in...*

She was doing it again. Letting herself be sucked into just gazing and gazing at him. She pulled back out again— out of the drowning emerald pool—with another straightening of her spine.

'Completion of the portrait will depend entirely on the number of sittings and the intervals between them. I understand it may well be irksome for you, but—'

Yet again, Guy de Rochemont effortlessly interrupted her determined reversion to the practicalities of immortalising him for his mother on canvas.

'So, tell me, Ms Harcourt, why should I select *you* for this task, in your opinion?'

The quizzical, questioning look was in his eye again. And something more. Something that Alexa found she didn't like. Up till now he had been the subject, she the observer—the riveted observer, unable to tear her eyes away from him. Now, suddenly, the tables were turned.

It was as if a veil had lifted from his eyes.

Emerald jewels...

Guy de Rochemont was looking at her. Straight at her. Unveiled and with full power.

It was heady, intoxicating—made her breathless! The words tumbled through the remains of her conscious mind, even as she felt the air catch in her throat.

Oh, good grief, he really is...

Attempts at analysis, classification, evaporated. They couldn't do anything else, because all she was capable of doing was sitting there, letting Guy de Rochemont look at her.

Assess her.

Because that was what he was doing. It came to her fuzzily, through the daze in her brain from the impact of those incredible green eyes resting on her. He was assessing her.

Rejection tightened through her. It was one thing for her to study *his* appearance—she was supposed to capture it on canvas! But it was quite another thing for him to subject her to the same scrutiny. And she knew just why he was doing it. For the same reason any man would do so. And when the man in question was someone like Guy de Rochemont, with a banking empire in his wallet and the looks of a film star, well—yes, he would think, wouldn't he, that he was entitled to evaluate her to that end?

Her mouth pressed together, and a spark showed in her eye. She suppressed it. She would not show she was reacting to him...to his uninvited scrutiny, she amended mentally. Because of course she was *not* reacting to him—not in any way other than to acknowledge, quite objectively, that his looks were exceptional, and that she needed to study them in order to paint them. That was all. *All.*

Yet again she recovered her composure, stifling her reaction to him, to those extraordinary eyes.

'That isn't a question for me to answer, Monsieur de Rochemont,' she responded. 'The selection of portraitist is entirely your own affair. If you wish to commission me, that is your privilege, and I will see whether my schedule is congruent with yours.'

She met his regard straight on. Her voice had been admirably crisp, which she was pleased about. All right, Guy de Rochemont was… Well, she wasn't about to run through the adjectives again—the evidence was right in front of her eyes! But that didn't mean she had to put up with being on the receiving end of his attention. Not that she had any reason to be concerned, anyway. There was only one outcome from his assessment. He would be seeing a plainly dressed, unadorned woman who was making not the slightest attempt to enhance her looks to please the male gender, and signalling thereby on all frequencies that she was not on any man's menu. Even that of a man who could quite clearly take his pick of the world's most beautiful women.

She wondered whether he would take offence at the way she'd responded to his question. Tough. She didn't need the commission, and if—and it was, she knew, a very big if—she took it and if—and that was probably an even bigger if, because a man like him wouldn't care to be answered off-handedly—he commissioned her anyway, she was most definitely *not* going to pander to the man. Yes, he would doubtless cancel sittings—because all her clients did to some extent or another—and that was understandable given the demands on his time because of his high-powered business life, and it was something she could cope with. But there was no way he was going to get the slightest pandering to, or her begging for the commission, or anything like that, thank you very much! She offered a service, a degree of skill and artistry. If a client wanted to buy it, that was that. If not—well, that was that too.

She met his gaze dispassionately as she finished speaking. For a moment he did not answer. She did not break her gaze, merely held his, looking untroubled and composed. The brilliance of his eyes seemed veiled somehow, as if he were masking something from her.

His reaction, she thought. *I can't tell whether he's annoyed, or indifferent, or what. I can't see into him.*

Again, it wasn't something that was unusual for her, given the calibre of her clients. Powerful men were not transparent to the world, and indeed that air of elusiveness, of restrained power, was something that usually went into her portraits—she knew, with a slight waspishness, that it was a form of flattery by her, to portray them as inscrutable.

But with Guy de Rochement the masking was, she felt, more pronounced. Perhaps it was because his was such a remarkably handsome face, so incredibly, overtly attractive to women. Women—any women—would expect to see some sort of reaction to them in his eyes, even if it were only polite indifference. But with Guy de Rochement nothing at all came through of what he was thinking.

She felt a tug of fascination go through her—the eternal fascination of an enigmatic man—and then, on its heels, a different emotion, a more chilling one.

He keeps apart. He holds back. He shows only what he wants to show, what is appropriate for the moment.

Then, abruptly, he was speaking again, and her attention went to what he was saying. What his face was suddenly showing.

She could see quite plainly what it was.

It was amusement.

Not open, not pronounced, but there all the same—in

the narrowing of his eyes, in the indentation of his sculpted lips. And more than amusement there was something else, just discernible to her. Slight but distinct surprise.

Alexa knew why. *He's not used to being answered like that—and not by a woman.*

She felt a sliver of satisfaction go through her. Then was annoyed with herself for feeling it. Oh, for heaven's sake, what did she care whether this man was or was not used to having someone answer him like that?

'You do not believe in pitching, do you, Ms Harcourt?' The subtly accented voice was dry.

Alexa gave the slightest shrug. 'To what purpose? Either you like my work and wish to engage me, or you do not. It's a very simple matter.'

'Indeed.' The voice was a dry murmur again. One narrow, long-fingered hand reached out to close around the stem of a martini glass and raise it contemplatively to his mouth, before lowering it to the table again. His regard was still impassively on her. Then, as if reaching a decision, he got to his feet.

Alexa did likewise. *OK*, she thought, *that's it. No deal. Well, so what? Imogen will be cross with me, but actually I'm glad he's decided against me.*

She wondered why she felt so certain of that, but knew she did. She'd work out later just what that reason was. Then it came to her.

Because it's simpler. Easier. More straightforward.

Yet even so she felt her mind sheering away. And necessarily so. Now was not the time to analyse why a feeling of relief was going through her *not* to be painting Guy de Rochement's portrait—or why the feeling running just beneath the surface of that relief was something quite, quite different.

Regret...

No! Don't be absurd, she admonished herself sternly. *It's just a commission, that's all. You've done dozens, and you'll do dozens more. Just because unlike all the others this one is young and ludicrously handsome, it means nothing at all. Nothing.*

He was speaking, and she cut short her futile cogitations.

'Well, Ms Harcourt, I think we have reached the end of our necessary exchange, don't you?'

Guy de Rochemont was holding his hand out to her. She made herself take it, ignoring the cool of his touch and dropping it again the moment social convention permitted.

'Quite,' she agreed crisply. She picked up her bag, ready to turn and leave.

'So,' Guy de Rochemont continued, 'I will have my PA phone your representative and arrange my first sitting—should it prove possible within the restraints of our respective diaries.' He paused a moment. Just the fraction of a moment. 'I trust that meets with your approval, Ms Harcourt?'

Was that amusement in his voice again? A deliberate blandness in his gaze? Alexa found her lips pressing together as her thoughts underwent a sudden and complete rearrangement.

'Yes—thank you,' she answered, and her voice, she was glad to hear, was as crisp as ever.

'Good,' said her latest client, as if the word closed the transaction. And then, as if Alexa had just ceased to exist, he looked past her. His expression changed.

'Guy! Darling!'

A woman sailed up to him, ignoring Alexa's presence as if she were invisible. A cloud of heavy scent surrounded the woman even as her slender braceleted arms came around Guy de Rochemont to envelop him. Alexa caught an impression of tightly sheathed black silk, long lush black hair, and a tanned complexion. Moreover, the woman's features were definitely familiar. Who was she? Oh, yes, Carla Crespi—that was it. An Italian *femme fatale* film actress who specialised in sultry roles. Alexa hadn't seen any of her films, as they weren't to her taste, but it would have been hard not to have heard of the woman at all.

She turned to go. It was par for the course that a male of Guy de Rochemont's calibre would have a woman like that in tow. Someone high-profile, high-maintenance, who would, above all, adorn him. A trophy woman for an alpha-plus male.

She heard the woman launch into a stream of rapid Italian, pitched too loud for private conversation and therefore, Alexa assumed, designed for public consumption—drawing attention to herself, to the man she was with. Tucking her handbag firmly under her arm, Alexa left her to it and departed.

She felt strangely disconcerted.

And it annoyed her.

She would have felt even more disconcerted, and certainly more annoyed, had she realised that behind her Guy de Rochemont had disengaged himself from Carla Crespi and was looking after Alexa's departing figure as she threaded her way across the room.

His eyes were very slightly narrowed and their expression was speculative. With just a hint—the barest hint—of amusement in their long-lashed emerald-green depths.

Imogen was, predictably, cock-a-hoop at Alexa's triumph. Not that Alexa saw it in that light at all—not even when Imogen disclosed the fee she had negotiated, which was considerably higher than Alexa had yet commanded.

'Didn't I tell you you'll be made after this?' Imogen demanded. 'You'll be able to name your own price, however stratospheric. It's all fashion—you know that!'

'Thank you,' Alexa said dryly. 'And there was I thinking it was my talent.'

'Yes, yes, yes,' said Imogen. 'But brilliant artists are ten a penny and starving in their garrets surrounded by their masterpieces. Look, Alexa, art is a *market*, remember? And you have to work the market, that's all. Stick with me and one day you'll be worth squillions—and so will I!'

But Alexa only shook her head lightly, and forebore to discuss a subject they would never see eye to eye on. Nor did she discuss her latest client, even though Imogen was ruthless in trying to squeeze every last detail out of her.

'Look, he's just what you said he was, all right? A jaw-droppingly fantastic-looking male, rich as Croesus. So what? What's that got to do with me? I'm painting him, that's all. He'll turn up late to sittings, cancel more than he makes, and somehow or other I'll get the portrait delivered, get my fee paid, and that will be an end of it. He's having the portrait done for his mother, and presumably it will hang in her boudoir, or the ancestral hall, or one of them. I don't know, and I don't care. I'll never see it again and that will be that.'

'Mmm,' said Imogen, ignoring the latter half of Alexa's pronouncement and rolling her eyeballs dreamily. 'All those one-on-ones with him. All that up-close-and-personal as he poses for you. All that—'

'All that cool, composed professional distance,' completed Alexa brusquely.

'Oh, come on, Alexa,' her friend cried exasperatedly. 'Don't tell me you wouldn't swoon if he made a pass at you. Of *course* you would—even you! Mind you...' Her eyes targeted Alexa critically. 'Dressed like that you won't get the chance!'

Precisely, thought Alexa silently. And anyway, not only was a man who had Carla Crespi panting for him never going to look twice at any other female, but—and this was the biggest but in the box—the only thing she was remotely interested in Guy de Rochemont for was whether she could successfully paint him.

The prospect was starting to trouble her. Up till now her main challenge had been not to make her sitters too aware of their physical limitations. With Guy de Rochemont it was a different ballgame. She found she was going over the problem in her head, calling his face into her mind's eye and wondering how she should tackle it. Wondering whether she could catch the full jaw-dropping quality of the man.

Will I be able to do him justice?

Doubts assailed her right from the start. As she had predicted, he missed the first sitting and was ninety minutes late for the next one. Yet when he did arrive his manner was brisk and businesslike, and apart from taking three mobile calls in succession, in as many languages, he let Alexa make her first preliminary sketches without interruption.

'May I see?' he said at the end, and his tone of voice told Alexa that this was not a request, despite the phrasing. Silently she handed across her sketchbook, watching his face as he flicked through her afternoon's work.

Pencil and charcoal were good media for him, she'd realised. They somehow managed to distil him down to his essence. Beginning full-on with oils would make his looks unreal, she feared. No one would believe a man could look that breathtaking. People would think she'd flattered him shamelessly.

But it was impossible to flatter Guy de Rochemont, she

knew. The extraordinary visual impact he'd had on her at her first encounter with him had not lessened an iota. When he'd walked into her studio earlier that afternoon she'd found, to her annoyance—and to quite another emotion she refused to call anything but her artistic instinct—that her gaze was, yet again, completely riveted to him. She simply could not tear her eyes away. She just wanted to drink him in, absorb every feature, every line.

When his mobile had rung, and with only the most cursory 'excuse me' he'd launched into French so fast and idiomatic it was impossible for her to follow a single word, she had actually welcomed the opportunity to resume her scrutiny of him. Unconsciously she'd found herself reaching for her sketchbook and pencil.

Now, as he flicked through her labours' fruits, she was watching him again. He definitely, she thought, had the gift of not showing his reaction. Whether he approved of what she'd done or not, she had no idea. Not that his disapproval would have bothered her in the least.

If he doesn't like what I produce, he can sack me, she thought, with a defiance she had never applied to her other clients.

But then never had she had a client like Guy de Rochemont.

As the sittings proceeded, intermittently and interrupted, as she knew they would—because his diary could alter drastically from day to day as with all such high-flyers who relied on others to accommodate themselves around them—she realised with what at first was nothing more than mild irritation that he started to disturb her. And it disturbed her that he disturbed her.

Even more that it was starting to show.

Oh, not to him. To him she was still able to keep entirely distanced during the sittings, to maintain a brisk, almost taciturn demeanour which, thankfully, mirrored his. He would usually arrive with a PA or an aide, with whom he more often than not maintained a flow of rapid conversation in a language Alexa did not understand, while the PA or aide took dictation or notes. Sometimes he took phone calls, or made them, and once he nodded a cursory apology to her when a second aide arrived with a laptop which he handed to his boss to peruse. After he had done so, Guy snapped it shut and resumed his pose again. Alexa coped with it all, and said nothing. She preferred not to speak to him. Preferred to keep any exchange to the barest functional minimum.

Yet it didn't help. Not in the slightest.

Guy de Rochemont still disturbed her in ways that she just did *not* want to think about.

Unfortunately, Imogen did. Worse—she revelled in it!

'Of *course* he's getting to you!' she trilled triumphantly. 'Otherwise you wouldn't snap when you say his name, or when I do. It's a sure sign.' She gave a gusty sigh. 'It's all totally theoretical, alas. He's all over Carla Crespi. She's preening herself rotten about it. Puts the pair of them in front of every camera she can find. Or buy. Even with your looks—if you bothered to do anything to show them off— you couldn't compete with her.'

Alexa tightened her jaw and refused to rise to the bait.

Besides, she had bigger problems than Imogen winding her up.

The portrait wasn't working.

It had taken her a while to realise it. At first she'd thought it was going well—the initial sketches had worked, the simple line drawing being ideal for catching the angled planes of that incredible face—but as she started to paint in oil, it didn't happen. At first she thought it was the medium, that oil was not the best for such a face. Then, after a while, it started to dawn on her, with a deep chill inside her, that the problem was not the medium. It was her.

I can't catch him. I can't get him down. I can't get the essence of him!

She took to staring, long after he had gone, at her efforts. She could feel frustration welling up in her. More than frustration.

Why can't I make this work? Why? What's going wrong?

But she got no answer. She tried at one point to make a fresh start, on fresh canvas, working from the initial sketches all alone at night in her studio. But her second attempt failed too. She stared, and glared, and then with dawning realisation knew that, however hard she tried, it was simply not going to work. She could not paint Guy de Rochemont.

Not from life, not from sketches, not from memory.

Nor from dreams.

Because that was the most disturbing thing of all. She'd started to dream about him. Dream of painting him. Disturbing, restless dreams that left her with a feeling of frustration and discomfort. At first she had told herself it was nothing more than her brain's natural attempt to come up with a solution that her waking mind and conscious artistry could not achieve. That dreaming of painting Guy de Rochement was simply a means to work through the inexplicable block she was suffering from.

But then, after the third time she'd dreamt of him, and woken herself from sleep with a jolt at the realisation that yet again he'd intruded into the privacy of her mind, she knew she'd have to throw in the towel and admit defeat.

It galled her, though—badly. It went against the grain to give up on a commission. She'd never done it before, and it was totally unprofessional. But it was also unprofessional to turn in substandard work. That broke every rule in her book. So, like it or not—and she didn't—she had no option. She was going to have to admit she couldn't do the portrait, and that was that.

Even so, it took time—and a lot of agonising—to bring herself to the point where she knew she would have to inform Guy de Rochemont of her decision. When to do it? And how? Wait until he turned up—eventually—for his next sitting, and then apologise in front of whichever of his staff were there with him that day? Or, worse, ask him for a word in private and then tell him? One cowardly part of her thought to let Imogen do it—after all, Imogen was her agent. But if there was one thing Alexa knew for sure, it was that Imogen would refuse to let her throw in the towel. No, she would just have to bite the bullet and do it herself, face to face. And it wasn't fair on the man to make him turn up for a sitting he scarcely had time for anyway and then tell him she was resigning the commission.

So she phoned his office instead.

The PA—whose manner had not improved—told her snootily that Mr de Rochemont was out of the country, and an appointment to see him was highly unlikely before the date of the next sitting. So Alexa was surprised when the PA rang back later, to tell her that it would be convenient for Guy to see Alexa in a week's time, at six in the evening. Alexa wanted to say that the time would not be in the least convenient for her, but forebore. This had to be done, and she wanted it over with.

When she turned up at the London headquarters of Rochemont-Lorenz, she was kept waiting in Reception for a good half an hour—not a surprise—and then finally taken up in a bronze-lined lift to the executive floor, some twenty storeys above Reception. Her feet sank into carpet an inch thick, and thence she went through huge mahogany double doors into the chairman's suite.

The setting sun was streaming in through plate glass windows.

Guy de Rochemont got to his feet from behind a desk that was the size of a car and about a tennis court's length from the entrance doors, and came forward.

'Ms Harcourt...'

His voice was smooth, his suit so immaculate that it clung to his lean, elegant body like a glove.

And yet again Alexa found herself gazing at him. Drinking him in. Feeling that incredible breathless rushing in her veins as she watched him cross the deep carpet, his gait lithe, purposeful, like a soft footed leopard.

Prince of the pride...

Thoughts, reactions, tumbled through her head as he came up to her.

This is his natural environment. Here in this penthouse, overlooking the City. With money and power and wealth and privilege. An ivory tower remote from the world. Where he reigns supreme, alone.

He had come right up to her, his long-fingered hand extended. Automatically she took it, wishing she did not have to, did not have to feel the cool strength in his brief social grip before he let her go.

He looked at her, studying her face a moment with a flicker of his eyes. The familiar thought stuttered through her brain.

Green eyes—as rich as emeralds... And lashes, those ridiculously long lashes, and that veiling I can't see through...

'Is there a problem?'

She stared. How had he known? She'd said nothing— nothing at all—of the problems she was having. She scarcely spoke to him during sittings, and thank heavens he had never asked to see her progress—not once she'd started on the oils. Nor had he made any comment at all on the initial pen-and-ink sketches. She'd been glad. She hadn't wanted his comment—hadn't wanted anything to do with him, if truth be told. She had been relieved that he wanted no conversation with her, that he was basically using her studio as an extension of his office. His preoccupation with his work meant she could study him, paint him in full concentration. Hiding completely the fact that she was utterly failing to capture his likeness—his essence—in a portrait.

For a moment she was stymied by his directness. Then, with a stiffening of her back, she answered, moving slightly away from him to increase the distance between them. It felt more comfortable that way.

'I'm afraid so,' she said. Her voice was stiff, but she couldn't help it. She was just about to tell a rich and influential client whose portrait was, as Imogen never failed to remind her, the gateway to unprecedented commercial success, that she was incapable of fulfilling the commission.

He raised a slightly, enquiring eyebrow, but said nothing. His eyes still had that veiling over them.

How's he going to take this? Finding out all that priceless time of his has been wasted, that there's nothing to show for it, and never will be? He's going to be livid!

For the first time she felt apprehensive—not because she was going to have to admit artistic failure, but because it was dawning on her that Guy de Rochemont could ruin her career. All he had to do was say that she was unreliable…

She took a deep breath. She owed him the truth, and could not put it off any longer. He was clearly waiting for her explanation. So she gave it.

'I can't paint you.'

His expression did not change. He merely paused, for a sliver of time so brief she hardly noticed, then said, his eyes resting on her, 'Why is that?'

'Because I can't,' said Alexa. She sounded an idiot, but couldn't help it. Couldn't explain. She took a breath, her voice sounding more clipped than politeness required. 'I can't paint you. I've tried and I've tried, and it's just not working. I'm extremely sorry but I have to resign the commission. I mustn't waste any more of your time.'

She waited for his reaction. It would not be pleasant—and who could blame him? His time was invaluable, and she'd wasted a great deal of it. She felt her shoulders squaring in preparation.

But his reaction was completely *not* what she had steeled herself for. He merely walked back to his desk, gestured to the huge leather executive chair slightly to one side of it, and then lowered himself down into his even huger chair behind the desk.

'Artist's block,' he said dismissively. *'N'inquietez vous.'*

Alexa could only stare.

'No,' she repeated, 'I really can't paint you. I'm extremely sorry.'

He smiled—a brief, social smile that barely indented his mouth. *'Pas de tout.* Please—won't you sit down? May I offer you some coffee? A drink, perhaps, as the sun has very nearly set?'

She didn't move. 'Mr de Rochemont, I really have to emphasise that I have no choice but to resign the commission. I can't paint you. It's impossible! Just impossible!'

She could hear her voice rising, and it dismayed her. She wanted to get out of here, but how could she? Guy de Rochemont was still indicating that she should come and sit down, and without knowing why she found that that was exactly what she was doing. She sat, almost with a bump, clutching her handbag.

'I can't paint you,' she said again.

His eyes were resting on her with that familiar veiled regard that she could not read in the slightest. 'Very well. If that is your decision I respect it entirely. Now, tell me, Ms Harcourt, do you have an engagement this evening?'

Alexa stared. What had *that* got to do with anything?

He took her silence for negation. 'Then I wonder,' he went on, his eyes never leaving her face, 'if it would be agreeable to you to be my guest this evening. I feel sure the event would be of interest to you. It is the private opening of the forthcoming exhibition on Revolution and Romanticism: Art in the Napoleonic Period. Rochemont-Lorenz has the privilege of being one of the key sponsors.'

Alexa went on staring. Then she said the first coherent thing that came into her head. 'I'm not dressed for the evening.'

Once more Guy de Rochemont gave a brief social smile.

'*Pas de probleme,*' he said.

And it wasn't.

There was, Alexa discovered over the course of the next hour, absolutely no problem at all in transforming her from someone who was wearing the same dull grey blouse and skirt that she'd worn the first time she'd encountered her client to someone who—courtesy of the use of the facilities of a penthouse apartment that seemed to form a substantial portion of the executive floor, plus a stylist who appeared out of nowhere with two sidekicks, hairdresser and make-up artist, and a portable wardrobe of eveningwear—looked astoundingly, shockingly different.

When she emerged, one hectic, extraordinary hour later, and walked into the executive floor reception area, Guy de

Rochemont looked up from where he'd been talking on the phone at the deserted secretarial desk and said only one thing to her.

His eyes—those green, inscrutable eyes—rested on her for only a brief moment. He took in the slender figure in raw silk—burnt sienna, with a high neckline but bare arms—her hair in a crown around her head and her face in full make-up, with eyes as deep as oceans.

Then he walked forward, stopped just in front of her.

'*At last.*'

That was all he said.

And he didn't mean how long she'd kept him waiting.

Satisfaction ran through Guy as he surveyed the woman in front of him. He had had more than ample time to peruse her attributes during his sittings, and Alexa Harcourt in evening attire was all that he wanted her to be.

Superbe.

The single adjective formed in his mind, and he plucked it from the list of many that he could apply to her and considered it. Yes, *superbe*…

Nothing less would do as a description. He had known from the first moment he'd laid eyes on her that once he'd disposed of the prim schoolteacher image she so amusingly put forward he would reveal for his delectation a beauty well worth his attention. And so it had proved.

His eyes rested on her appreciatively. Yes, *superbe* indeed. Tall, graceful, slender, with that classic English chic—so understated, yet so powerfully alluring for that very reason—she was exactly what he wanted her to be. A wisp of a smile played at his lips as he called to mind the muted, self-effacing persona she had presented up to this point. At first he had assumed it was a ploy, for women went to vast efforts to engage his interest, and she would not have been the first to attempt a pose of indifference to him. But as the sittings had continued he had come to the conclusion—surprising, but for that very reason enticing— that Alexa Harcourt was *not* courting his interest.

Not, of course, that she was not all too aware of him. That had been evident to him from the first, and it had come to be a source of amusement to him, adding a rare piquancy to his pursuit—a pursuit which he had taken considerable enjoyment in extending for far longer than he customarily did when it came to the women he selected for his relaxation. But he had found that it was *fort amusant* to sit, posed like a prince in his Renaissance palace, while his portrait was captured for posterity—or in his case for his fond *maman*—and let his eyes play over her sculpted features. He found pleasure in this casual scrutiny, while she assiduously endeavoured to ignore his regard.

But not without revealing by her very assiduity just how responsive she was increasingly becoming to his presence.

His eyes veiled momentarily. That increasing responsiveness was evidently, the reason why she had come here to make her dramatic announcement that she could not continue with making his portrait. Again, at first for a few moments he had assumed she had done so merely to put to the test whether he was or was not interested in her. But then he had realised, with a sense of relief as well as satisfaction, that his reading of her was unchanged—she was quite genuine in her determination to abandon his portrait.

It was an excellent sign! Excellent that she was not attempting to be *intrigant*, but even more excellent that she was having such problems with the task of capturing his likeness. Because the reason for that was obvious—he was no longer nothing more than a client to her. And most essential of all, her inability to capture his likeness betokened her increasing frustration at her own attraction to him. She could not paint him….because she could only desire him.

And desire was exactly what he felt for her. He had experienced it the moment he'd realised how much of a front her austere appearance and repressive manner was. He had allowed himself the luxury of a slow, enjoyable cultivation of his desire. Now, as she stood before him in the rich, lustrous beauty she was finally revealing to him, his desire rose pleasurably. Anticipation speared within him for what he knew would be the delights of the evening—the night—ahead.

Not that she gave any sign yet of realising what was to happen. She was, he knew, quite unconscious of what lay ahead with absolute inevitability. How was it, he found himself wondering with amusement, that she could be so unaware of it? He knew of no other woman who would not have realised long before that he was interested in her. But then, he mused, that was part of her allure.

It would, of course, make her seduction even more *piquant*—even more enticing!

And now the evening was about to begin.

'Shall we?' he invited.

He ushered her to the door, and across the now-deserted reception area of the executive floor. She walked with superb grace, his appreciative eye noted, although there was the very slightest tension in her shoulders. As if she were not entirely at her ease.

But of course she would not be. She was still, *évidemment*, quite *bouleversé*, by the unexpectedness of the situation. Yet striving to carry it off all the same—as if she had quite expected to be gowned and coiffed and taken off to a gala soirée. It amused him to think it was her oh-so-English *sang-froid* that was allowing her to be so matter-of-fact about it.

On their descent to the underground car park lot in his personal elevator, he chatted inconsequentially about the forthcoming event. She made the appropriate responses, civil and unexceptional, and in that manner they gained the waiting limo, its engine purring as they emerged. He guided her into its interior and followed likewise, giving the signal to his chauffeur to proceed.

The journey was a bare fifteen minutes, if that, to the West End, and in the car he continued with his inconsequential chat. But it was sporadic only, and he was pleased. It was good to know that she was not one of those tiresome women who felt impelled to chatter the whole time. Alexa's reserve won his approval, as did her obvious ability to travel without incessant talking. Instead, she seemed perfectly content merely to make whatever appropriate comment was required to answer his remarks, being neither taciturn nor garrulous.

He liked that, he decided. And, moreover, he liked the opportunity it gave him, as she gazed composedly out of the tinted windows at the passing London scene, to let his regard appreciate her fully, her profile averted, and all her graceful figure displayed to him at his leisure.

Yes, she was indeed well worth his time and attention. Pleased with his choice, he relaxed fully into the leather seats and continued his appreciative surveillance. The evening stretched pleasurably ahead of him.

And the night—ah, the night would be exceptional...

Dim daylight was pressing at Alexa's eyelids. Slowly, as if lifting a weight, she opened her eyes. Taking in her surroundings.

It was a hotel bedroom. A hotel whose famous name

alone was synonymous with style, exclusiveness and luxury. A hotel in which she had dined the previous evening, in a suite larger than her apartment, at a dining table resplendent with silver and napery around which had been seated half a dozen couples, all guests at the highly prestigious art gallery earlier in the evening, all of whom, so it appeared, had been invited to dine with Guy de Rochemont. Along with herself.

Precisely how that had come about she had not quite understood—only that Guy de Rochemont had taken her elbow as the reception ended and guided her back into the chauffeured limo. They'd been disgorged a short while later into the lobby of the hotel, and then she'd been swept up with the other arriving dinner guests to the penthouse floor and into this suite.

There had seemed to be no good opportunity to take her leave, and instead she had found herself being seated at the dinner table along with the others. At that point she had acquiesced as composedly as she could, and accepted that her presence at Guy de Rochemont's side must be for the same reason he had taken her to the opening.

And that could only be, Alexa had mused, trying to make sense of his extraordinary behaviour, because his preferred partner—surely the exotic Carla Crespi still?—had for whatever reason not been available, and he must have assumed that the exhibition would be of intrinsic artistic interest to her as a portraitist. Indeed it had been, despite her acute consciousness of the disturbing presence of Guy de Rochemont at her side.

Because disturbing it most definitely was. She had done her best to ignore his presence, but Guy de Rochemont was difficult to ignore at all times, and the sleek dark sheath of a tuxedo made it completely impossible. But her mounting consciousness of him should—*must*! she had thought—be utterly suppressed. Whatever the reason she could not complete his portrait, whatever the reason for her quite inappropriate consciousness of him all evening, the only reaction to him she must show was none at all. She must be cool, she must be composed, she must be an unobtrusive guest and nothing more.

Her dogged composure had held through the meal, even through the ritual of serving coffee and liqueurs in the suite's sitting room, but as the guests had taken their leave she had found it difficult, yet again, to time the moment of announcing her own departure. So, to her consternation, as the last couple had left, she'd been left with Guy de Rochemont *à deux*.

Instantly, without the social conversation of the other guests, the atmosphere had seemed to change—though she'd known it was nothing more than her own resurgent consciousness of him. Definitely time to take her leave and remove herself from what had been a very taxing evening. It had been considerate of her august client not to be annoyed at her resigning his commission, gracious of him to invite her to an exhibition she would be professionally interested in, and courteous of him to include her in his dinner party, despite her having no claim whatsoever to be there. But the dinner party had been over, and it had been time for her to go. Time for her to regain the soothing sanctuary of her flat. Time to put her brief, professionally based acquaintance—nothing more than that!—with Guy de Rochemont behind her.

With that purpose clear, she had taken a breath, put a polite smile on her face

'I really must go,' she said, her voice admirably controlled, she was glad to note. Though she had partaken only frugally of alcohol, champagne had circulated at the exhibition and an array of wines had been poured at dinner, so she was aware that she had consumed sufficient if not for intoxication, then for a discernible weakening of her normal composure.

She got to her feet, feeling the column of silk slide down her body as she moved. Felt it disconcertingly, as if her body had somehow become as ultra-conscious as her mind…

'Of course,' said Guy de Rochemont, getting to his feet as well.

Involuntarily, Alexa's eyes went to him.

The stark austerity of his evening dress etched him against the paleness of the decor, emphasised the flawless planes of his face, the extraordinary green eyes beneath the dark winged brows, the sable hair.

For one hapless fraction of a second she could not move her gaze. Could only remain standing there, with supreme consciousness of that arresting physical presence that drew all eyes quite helplessly. She could not drag her gaze from him. Her body seemed inert immobile, beyond her control. Then, wresting back her control with intense effort, she veiled her eyes and started to walk towards the door. Getting out of here was a priority. A necessity.

But as she gained the door Guy de Rochemont was before her, tall, and dark and dominating her senses. With a rigid stiffening of her spine she turned, holding out her hand, the gesture determinedly final.

'Thank you so much for this evening, Mr de Rochemont. I enjoyed it so much. It was extremely kind of you to invite me.'

Her voice was cool, her tone restrained, her manner formal—as befitted the situation. She was a guest—unexpectedly so, given the vastly different world she moved in from the gilded orbit that Guy de Rochemont inhabited—thanking her host for his hospitality.

For a moment she could see something flickering in those incredible eyes. It seemed to be amusement. But it was also something else. Something that suddenly, belatedly, sent a dart quivering along her nerve fibres. Then he was responding to her polite, formal leavetaking.

'It was my pleasure,' murmured her host. 'And this,' he continued, somehow closing the gap between them, 'is an even greater pleasure...'

His smooth, long-fingered hand slid around the nape of her neck, the other hand took hers, twining his fingers between hers to draw her to him. His mouth dipped to hers. For a fraction of a second shock, sheer and undiluted, sheeted through her. Then a completely different sensation took over....

It was like nothing she had ever experienced! She had been kissed before, of course she had, but nothing, ever like this...

The lightest, most velvet touch, the merest grazing of his lips on hers, the most subliminal pressure of the tip of his finger moving in the delicate fronds of her hair at that most sensitive point on her nape. She felt her body start to weaken, her pulse quicken, and her conscious mind simply dissolve.

Slowly, very, very slowly, his kiss deepened.

And the last dissolving vestiges of her conscious mind left her.

And then, some completely indeterminable amount of time later, by some quite unaccountable means which she could never afterwards explain, she dimly realised that she was no longer standing by the door, but was instead—quite mysteriously—in a room that was dominated by a vast brocaded bed. Onto the broad expanse of this bed she was being effortlessly lowered, and slowly, very slowly and expertly, being made love to by Guy de Rochemont.

And there was nothing, absolutely nothing, that she could do about it—because with every cell in her body she realised it was the most exquisite thing that had ever happened to her...

Now, as she gazed out into the dimness of the hotel room, the night gone and day come again, her conscious mind came into residence after its extraordinary absence all through the long, dissolving night. She felt incredulity open within her.

How had it happened? How had it *possibly* happened? Disbelief was still echoing through her. How *could* she be in bed with Guy de Rochement? It was impossible! Just impossible!

Except that it wasn't.

It didn't take the evidence of her eyes to tell her that.

No, her whole body could bear testimony...

Memory shimmered through her every cell. Memory of sensations so exquisite, so extraordinary that they, too, could surely not be real. Except they were...

Hands—cool, fleeting—grazing along her bared arms. The tips of long fingers slow-running along the striations of her skin. Lips as soft as velvet playing over the contours of her body so that her whole being became a symphony of sensations—sensations that she had not known a body could experience. Light, questing fingertips exploring every curve, every secret sensual place, and lips tasting and arousing—oh, arousing! The swell of her breasts to coral peaks, which he savoured and engorged. Then his lips brushing down over her satin flesh. He had parted her loosening thighs and with a touch like silk prepared her for his possession.

She felt her body flush with warmth evoked by the humid, arousing memories.

How had it been possible to feel such sensation? It

was beyond imagining! Beyond everything except experience. An experience that was completely beyond her comprehension.

I never knew! Never dreamed it could be like that—never!

Wonder soared through her, increasing her bemusement, her incomprehension of how this had come to be, her presence here. She knew with a frail, wavering fragment of her normal self that what she had done had been not only inexplicable, but total and complete folly—to have fallen into bed with Guy de Rochemont could be nothing else! Yet right now, as she lay cocooned at his side, there was nothing more she could do, than acknowledge these truths. She knew that if she had any vestige of sanity left she should leap from the bed, bundle herself into her clothes—*his* clothes—the clothes that he had first dressed her in then taken off her—and rush out of the hotel as fast as decorum could take her.Yet she could not do so. Not because it wasn't the sane thing to do, but because her body seemed so strangely, uncommonly inert…languorous…

That sense of wonder, mixed now with a strange new sense of extraordinary well-being, suffused her body and her mind, making her feel slumberous, supine. And now something else came over her—an overwhelming urge to turn her head, to see the man who had accomplished her presence at his side.

Slowly she tilted her head, and as her eyes lit upon his face she felt something very strange lift inside her—just the slightest ripple, as if a light breeze had moved across still, untouched water, setting in motion something she did not know. She could not tell what it might be—some ineffable current that might take her she knew not where? As her eyes came to rest on the face of the man lying beside her she felt again wonder and bemusement—and more.

She felt her breath catch. Dear God, the man was perfection! That face that she had drawn so often, sketching over and over again to try and capture its essence, that she had tried frustratingly, so frustratingly, to translate into paint on canvas, riveted her gaze.

She had never been so close to it—to him. The sense of intimacy overwhelmed her—that she should be centimetres away from him, their limbs still half entwined. His face was so close that all she had to do was lift her hand, as she found herself now doing without conscious volition, and brush with the lightest touch the lock of satin hair across his forehead. She gazed at the long lashes of his eyes, swept down over the sculpted plane of his cheek.

He was deeply asleep—she could see the steady, rhythmic rise and fall of his chest, see the pulse at his throat, feel the warmth of his breath on her hand. As she touched him he did not stir, and she was glad—for she wanted only this moment now, gazing at the extraordinary perfection of his face, a homage to male beauty that for this one night had out of nowhere been a gift of fortune to her.

And that was what it had been, she knew. Whatever the reason Guy de Rochemont had chosen not to send her home but to take her here instead, she knew it was no more than a passing appetite, no more than filling an empty night with someone who, for a night at least, was worthy of his possession however fleeting his desire for her. Yet it felt like a gift. She felt it with every sensuous memory still warming her body, flushed with the heat of their congress.

I was mad to let it happen! But it did, and I cannot regret it—not now, not here. I can regret it later, tomorrow—all those tomorrows—and think how weak and foolish I was. But for now, for this day, I cannot regret it.

A smile played at her mouth. Yes, she had been foolish beyond belief, foolish and weak, but what had happened she could not regret—not with her body whispering to her in every cell just how transformed she was. Her eyes softened as her gaze stayed upon that perfect face, displayed for her in deep repose.

Cliché it might be, but any woman chosen by Guy de Rochemont must surely take away from the encounter only her appreciation

'*Ma belle…*'

He had awakened, his eyes holding hers immediately, the intimacy of his gaze at once drawing her to him. As her eyes twined with his she started to drown in their green long-lashed depths, as if there were no more air to breathe in the world.

He kissed her, their mouths mingling, and a sweetness went through her that warmed her body. As he drew away his eyes were tinged with regret.

'*Hélas*—I cannot do what you must know I long to do. I cannot stay. *Je suis désolé.*'

With a single fluid movement he stood up out of the bed, supremely unconscious of his nakedness—and of his condition. Alexa could feel her cheeks flush as she realised.

'Yes,' he allowed ruefully, 'I do not need to lie to you—I would give much, *ma belle*, to stay. But it cannot be. So I must ask you only to excuse my neglect.'

He turned away, walking into the en suite bathroom, and a moment later Alexa heard the rushing of water as the shower started. For one timeless moment she lay there, feeling out of nowhere a desolation that was far beyond the polite utterance he had made on his own behalf. It was only for a fraction of a second, but it was like the tip of a whip across her heart.

No!

Where the admonition came from she didn't know. She only knew that it was essential that she administer it.

Essential, too, to take instant advantage of this window of opportune solitude. She threw back the bedclothes and stood up. Again, for a moment, she felt her body was different somehow—changed—but then she thrust the moment aside, casting around to see where her clothes might be. Gathering them up, she hastily got herself dressed. It seemed absurd—more than absurd—to be putting on evening clothes again, but there was nothing else to be done. As she finished zipping up the elegant, beautifully made dress—whose price was beyond her range even at her most self-indulgent!—a sudden depression of the spirits crumpled her. She shut her eyes. Hot chagrin burned her cheeks. Suddenly the sordidness of her situation hit her.

A one-night stand—that was what she had been. A passing convenience, a handy female—good enough to fill the night hours of a man who kept company with film stars, who'd dressed her up to his standard. And now, her purpose fulfilled, she had only to cover her nakedness and remove herself.

No! It hadn't been like that—it hadn't! Not for her, at least. She wouldn't let such thoughts intrude, wouldn't let the wonder of it all warp into something sordid and regrettable. Because it hadn't been! Yes, of *course* she was simply a passing fancy. How could she be anything but to a man like Guy de Rochemont? But that didn't mean it had been tacky or repellent. Every portion of her body told her otherwise.

She took a deep breath, straightening her shoulders. The beautiful line of the gown shimmered over her body, reminding her of how she had looked last night. With swift fingers she reached into the tumbled mass of her hair and plaited her tresses into a long pigtail over one shoulder, glancing in one of the many wardrobe mirrors as she did so. Yes, that was fine. Neat, tamed. Her eyes were still smudged with make-up, but a quick wipe with a tissue from the vanity unit removed a great deal—enough until she could gain her own flat. Slipping her feet into the soft leather shoes, she reached for the evening purse that went with the gown. There—she was ready to go.

Calm and composed again.

The door of the bathroom opened and Guy de Rochemont emerged, his showered body clad now in a dazzling white hotel bathrobe. His sable hair was damp, and diamond drops dewed his long eyelashes. Alexa felt her breath catch, felt a sense of wonderment that for a few brief hours he had been hers to embrace.

Well, now it was the morning, and real life took over again. *His* would, clearly, and so must hers.

'*Cherie*, there was no rush for you!' His voice was amused, as well as rueful, as he took in her dressed state at a glance as he strode to the wardrobes and threw open the doors. Inside, Alexa caught a glimpse of serried male garments hanging up. 'You should have stayed in bed—had breakfast. It is only I who had to make this infernal early departure—*tant pis*!'

'No, that's quite all right.' Alexa's voice was composed, beautifully composed, and she was proud of herself. As if there was nothing extraordinary about standing there in Guy de Rochemont's London hotel suite as he proceeded to get dressed. 'I must get going myself. I'll have the dress and accessories cleaned and returned. Should they go to your London offices, or...'

He gave her a questioning look as he shrugged himself into a pristine shirt. 'You don't like the dress? You should have said last night—the stylist would have found another for you. But I can assure you it suits you completely—you look *superbe* in it.' His voice changed a fraction. 'Just as I knew you would.'

'The dress doesn't belong to me,' she answered.

'Don't be absurd.' There was a flash of something that might be hauteur or irritation in his voice.

'Monsieur de Rochemont—' Alexa began. She hadn't actually intended to call him by his French name, but it had come out of her mouth automatically—out of habit.

His eyes flashed with green incredulity.

'*Monsieur?*' he echoed, his fingers stilling in the act of doing up his shirt. He stared at her. Then his mouth gave a wry smile. 'Alexa, I know you are English, and the English are very formal, but we have reached the point of first names—*je t'assure!*'

His clearly deliberate use of the intimate form of speech emphasised his assurance. She gave a slightly awkward lift of her hand. 'Well, it doesn't really matter anyway,' she said, 'since we shan't be seeing each other again. So—'

'*Comment?*' His expression froze.

Alexa's sense of awkwardness increased. 'I'm afraid I can't resume your commission…' she began, then trailed off, not actually wanting to put it into words. *Just because I've slept with you…*

He seemed to appreciate her unspoken point. Or at any rate ignore it. He gave a frown, as though something was not understood on her part.

'*N'importe pas.* The matter of the portrait, *cherie*, we can discuss later. However, the matter of moment now is that for some reason I have yet to comprehend you seem to think we "shan't be seeing each other again."' He echoed the intonation of her earlier words. '*Dis moi,*' he said, and his intonation changed again suddenly, as did the expression in his eyes, which all at once seemed to make Alexa's breathing stop. 'Did you find last night not to your liking?'

His voice—and his eyes—told her he knew the question

was as impossible to answer in the negative as if he had asked whether a rare vintage champagne might not be to her liking. Alexa made herself breathe.

'That isn't really the point,' she began, then stopped. She seemed to be beginning a lot of sentences and then stopping, not knowing how to proceed.

But her hesitation did not trouble Guy de Rochemont. He had resumed buttoning his shirt, and Alexa found her eyes going to the strong column of his throat, the lean twist of his wrists. Found her pulse somehow more noticeable. She really had to go—she really did. But Guy de Rochemont was saying something that brought her up short.

'*Bon.* Then we are agreed. Last night was exceptional, and we shall arrange matters accordingly. As I said, I am *désolé* that I am required to be on a pernicious flight to a tedious destination within the hour, but I shall return at the earliest moment—tonight, I hope. If not, then tomorrow at the latest. If you phone the London office my PA will give you my contact details for your convenience.'

He moved on to do up his cuffs, with swift, assured movements, then took out a tie and proceeded to knot it, continuing to talk to her as he did so. 'I shall endeavour to keep you apprised of my movements, but I must ask you to understand—as I am sure you do will—that I have commitments it is impossible for me to ignore, however much I may wish to do so. Accordingly, it is inevitable that there will be times—*hélas*—when I cannot honour my undertakings to you. I must therefore request your forbearance.'

He continued without a beat as he lifted his suit jacket from its padded hanger and shrugged himself into it, with an ease of movement she was burningly familiar with from all his sittings for her in her studio. 'Nevertheless, I trust we shall be able to spend sufficient time together, and that your work will permit you the flexibility required to ensure that. Have no anxieties for the moment. All can be arranged. For now, however...' He finished his knot, crossed to the bedside to retrieve the slim gold watch, wrapping it around his wrist as casually as if it had not been an item of masterly workmanship, with a price tag of several tens of thousands of pounds. 'I must fly to Geneva, and that is that. Already *le temps presse*, so I must ask your indulgence of my unseemly haste.'

He crossed towards her, buttoning his jacket as he did so, and Alexa found her hand being taken.

'Don't look so bemused, *ma belle.*' There was amusement in his voice, and a timbre that yet again seemed to make her breath catch. *'Tout sera bien. Tu vas voire.'*

He dropped the swiftest, most fleeting kiss on her mouth. As he started to move away, letting go of her hand to head for the door of the suite, she blurted out, her incomprehension evident in her voice, 'I don't understand!'

He paused by the door, in the act of opening it, and glanced back at her. Amusement was still in his eyes. That and something more—something that suddenly made Alexa's legs unable to support her.

'But it is very simple, *ma belle*—now we are lovers, *non*?'

And with that he was gone.

Behind him, staring blindly at the closed door, Alexa felt her mind go completely blank.

CHAPTER TWO

HER mind stayed blank all the way back to her apartment in the taxi she had climbed into at the hotel. She had walked with head held rigid across the marbled foyer, convinced that every eye in the hotel must be on her, seeing what she had done—for why else would a woman be leaving a hotel in the morning, still wearing the dress of the night before? She was sure, too, that the taxi driver had glanced knowingly at her in his mirror, and for that reason she'd stared blankly out of the window, before handing him a ten-pound note for her fare and walking into her apartment block as quickly as she could. She half ran up the stairs before any other occupant could spot her and jump to exactly the same conclusion. She had never done anything like this before—*never!*

'Well, of course you haven't!' she admonished herself as she gained the sanctuary of her bedroom and started to rid herself of the betraying dress. 'You've never been seduced by the likes of Guy de Rochemont before!'

But I have now...and I will remember it all my life.

Out of nowhere, she felt weak. She sank down on the bed, the reality of what had happened hitting her. Emotion came from all over—some that sense of wondrous bemusement, the almost physical memory of the hours entwined with him, and some sheer amazement about what had happened.

Playing over and over in her mind were the words he had left her with...

'Now we are lovers, non?'

Her expression changed. Confusion and incomprehension were in her eyes. What did he mean? What *could* he mean?

She found out within the hour. She had scarcely finished showering and changing her out-of-place evening gown for sensible daywear before her entryphone sounded. Heading downstairs to the entrance lobby, she discovered a delivery of flowers so huge that she could hardly carry them up to her flat. Inside, she fumbled for the note.

'À bientôt.'

It was all it said. All it needed to say. The phone call that came from Guy de Rochemont's PA five minutes later said the rest. The woman's dismissive style had not changed, but this time, instead of informing Alexa as she usually did that Mr de Rochemont either would or would not attend the next scheduled sitting, Alexa was given a mobile phone number 'as Mr de Rochemont instructed'. She was to use it instead of the London number, but only in reply to a call from its owner, and on no account must the number be made available to any other individual.

The woman finished with an admonitory flourish.

'Please ensure you do *not* call me, Ms Harcourt, in relation to Mr de Rochemont's itinerary. It will not be in my power to give you any information Mr de Rochemont has not instructed me to forward to you. Such information will be disclosed to you only on an "as necessary" basis, as Mr de Rochemont instructs.'

After the call, which Alexa had heard out in a silence that was partly due to her continuing inability to believe what she was hearing and partly because she had long since decided to ignore the woman's pointedly unpleasant manner, Alexa resumed her task of distributing the flowers into a variety of containers—for she possessed no single vase that was capable of holding the vast bouquet.

The scent of the flowers seemed overpowering. But her mind seemed strangely blank—as if too much had happened, too fast, and she could make no sense of it at all.

I don't know what to do, she thought. *I don't know what to do.*

Then don't do anything.

The words formed in her mind and brought a kind of relief. After all, nothing was required of her for the moment other than to place the vases around the flat. Then, knowing she was in no state of mind to go to her studio—where, anyway, no current commission awaited her other than Guy de Rochemont's, which, whatever the extraordinarily unbelievable events of the night before, she had resigned—she settled down at the desk in her living room and worked her way through a considerable amount of domestic paperwork, from utility bills to ongoing business expenses.

Then she vacuumed the flat, cleaned the kitchen, did some laundry and finally, after a light lunch, set off to the shops, having first despatched by courier the dress and accessories from last evening, with a note apologising because they had not been first cleaned, to Rochemont-Lorenz.

Her fridge restocked, she decided it would be a good opportunity to go to the gym, and spent several hours there. The exercise helped occupy her mind. Stop it falling back into vivid memory or that sense of blank incomprehension that seemed to be paralysing her brain. Back home again, she stayed in all evening, reading or watching back-to-back documentaries on television, before retiring to bed.

As she slipped between cool sheets she had a sudden searing memory of the previous night. For a moment she froze as heat flushed through her body. Then, with a decisive flick of the duvet, she reached for a book on early Italian art—her current bedtime reading. Pictures of martyred medieval saints would be an effective antidote to that betraying sensual flush—and to thoughts about the man who had caused it.

But about Guy de Rochemont she still didn't know what to do.

*I don't understand…*was her last conscious thought as sleep took her.

It was also her first conscious thought four days later, after days spent resuming her life as much as she was able, given her state of mental bemusement. She had come to the conclusion that the complete lack of any further communication by anyone remotely to do with Guy de Rochemont, let alone himself, could betoken only one thing: his parting words to her, the vast bouquet he had sent and the call from his PA with his private phone number, had not in fact meant anything. It was all beyond her comprehension, and continued to be so right up to the moment when, one Sunday, as she was passing a leisurely morning, the entryphone sounded.

It was Guy de Rochemont.

Numbly, she let him in. Numbly, she opened her front door to him. Numbly, she heard her own voice on her lips— 'I don't understand…'

He glanced down at her, wry amusement in his beautiful green long-lashed eyes that made her breath slow and her pulse instantly quicken. 'I told you, *ma si belle* Alexa, it is very simple. As simple…' he lowered his mouth to hers and took her into his arms '…as this.'

And so, over the next weeks, and then months, it seemed to be.

Without any conscious decision on her part, Alexa simply accepted the situation. Slowly, the sense of bemusement that it was happening at all seeped away, and having Guy de Rochemont in her life became just—well, her *life*. She did not look for words to describe it, she didn't want to—she didn't want to think about it either. It was simpler that way.

Simpler to accept this inexplicable affair. Simpler not to question him, or herself, or wonder why it was happening. For reasons known only to himself Guy de Rochemont wanted this. Why, she could not fathom. Carla Crespi seemed to be no longer on his radar. Alexa knew this from seeing a photo in a celebrity magazine of the sultry Italian star hooked onto the arm of a paunchy middle-aged man—a film director, according to the caption, which described him as Carla's fiancé. Had she defected? Had Guy tired of the actress? Alexa did not know. Did not want to ask.

Asking Guy about his life was something she refrained from doing. Again, why she was not entirely sure. One element, she knew, was because his existence away from her seemed so completely different from her life that she preferred not to think about it. Another reason was because she knew, with finely honed instinct, that Guy did not want to talk about his life.

Sometimes it overlapped into their time together, with a phone call to his mobile which he would take, talking in one of several European languages, and sometimes in English too. She caught snatches of conversation, but always busied herself, even if it were only to pick up a book or a newspaper while he was occupied.

Sometimes the tone of his voice, whatever language he was speaking, sounded impatient and irritated, his manner abrupt and peremptory. Then, phone call terminated, so too would be that attitude, and he was his usual self with Alexa again—relaxed and attentive, and, in bed, passionate and demonstrative.

Yet there was a reserve about him that she recognised—recognised because it resonated with her own innate reserve. A reserve that made her glad, too, that Guy showed no inclination to socialise with her, take her out and about. She was relieved, appreciative of his discretion—she had no wish to be seen as Guy de Rochemont's latest paramour, with curious, speculative eyes upon her, and besides, her time with him was too thinly spaced for her to want to spend it anywhere but in his private, exclusive company—wherever that was. Sometimes it was in her apartment, or he'd whisk her to where he was, where his punishing timetable permitted him her company. For time with Guy was precious—and scarce.

And it would not last for ever.

Could not.

The knowledge sent chill fingers creeping over her, and with it another sort of knowledge that seeped into her like icy drops.

How it had happened, she did not know. Why it had happened, she could not tell. That it had happened at all filled her with a terrible sense of both inevitable heartache and yet present rapture too.

For somewhere along the way—unintended, unimagined—she had done what she had never dreamt she would do. She had fallen in love with Guy de Rochemont.

Doomed, hopeless love. For there could be no future

with him, no ending other than the one she knew must come—one day the affair that had started so inexplicably would end, and Guy de Rochemont would no longer be part of her life. He would tire of her, move on, and she would be left behind.

Left behind loving him. Helplessly loving him. Hopelessly loving him.

The knowledge dismayed her—but it did not lessen by one fraction of a fragment the power of the truth about what she felt for Guy. A truth that she knew, with every instinct in her body, she must mask from him, and even, as best she could, from herself. That mask was all the protection she would have—a mask of cool composure that had once been the reality of her emotion but was now no more than a frail, flimsy disguise.

She needed it right up to the final moment when, out of the blue, the blow that she had known must fall one day fell.

Guy was leaving her. Ending their affair.

It was over.

CHAPTER THREE

SHE could not go on cleaning the bathroom for ever. After some indefinite time she made herself stop. Made herself go into the kitchen and put on the kettle. Carefully not looking at the breakfast table. Not thinking about what had happened that morning. Not thinking at all.

Just feeling.

An ocean of emotion possessed her.

After a while—a few minutes, an hour? She didn't know, couldn't tell and didn't care—she started to make herself think. Started to try and seize the torn and tattered rags of her mind and sew them back together again—at least enough to make words come, make words take shape in her head. She had to force herself to say them, if only to herself.

You knew this day would come. You knew it. You knew it had to come—could only come. You understood nothing of why he started this affair with you—what made you his choice. He, who had all the world to choose from. You understood nothing of that. Nothing of why he kept the affair going. The reasons must have been there, but they were inexplicable to you. You always knew that he would at some point, a point of his own choosing, decide to terminate the affair. End it. Finish it.

You knew it would happen.

And now it has.

You have done all that you could do, all that it was essential for you to do. You accepted its ending with dignity, with composure, with your mask intact. So that never could he possibly know the truth—the truth that he can have no interest in. Because why should he? Whatever he was to me, he was not a man it was...sensible...to fall in love with.

No... The word tolled in her brain. It had not been *sensible* to fall in love with Guy de Rochemont.

It had been folly of the worst sort. A folly she now had to pay the price for.

And she *would* pay that price.

She had accepted his severing of whatever it was that had been between them with composure and dignity. That was essential. Quite essential. She stood stock still in the kitchen, instilling into herself just how essential it was.

The phone started ringing.

For a moment she could only stare at it. A name, unspoken, was vivid in her head. Then, knowing that it was not Guy—for why should he phone now that he had ended the affair as abruptly as he had started it?—she jerked her hand to pick it up.

'Alexa! I've just found something out that I *must* warn you about! You've got to listen to me on this!'

Imogen's voice sounded agitated. For a moment Alexa could not face taking the call. But she knew she would not be able to avoid Imogen.

'What is it?' she answered. Her voice was as composed as Imogen's was not.

'I don't want to tell you this—I really, really don't! But I can't *not*—it's about Guy.'

Of course it was about Guy. How could it not be?

It was so ironic, Alexa thought dispassionately. From

being someone who couldn't have waxed any more lyrical about the attractions of Guy de Rochemont, lavish in her appreciation of all his masculine allure, Imogen had become the very opposite.

When she had first discovered the fact that Alexa had succumbed to him, Imogen's initial disbelief had been overwhelmed by a vicarious but wholehearted gratification.

'*Oh-my-God!* Are you serious? You and Guy de Rochemont! Oh, that is just *brilliant*! Wow! It's amazing! Awesome! Totally brilliant!' Imogen had enveloped her in a bear hug. 'Oh, you are just *so*, so lucky! You jammy, jammy thing!'

But her views had changed completely as she came to know the circumstances of their affair.

'It's like he's *hiding* you!' she'd accused. 'Never being seen out with you!'

Alexa had been unperturbed by her friend's hostility. 'The last thing I want is anyone staring at us,' she'd said. 'Besides, we don't get much time together—why waste it going out? I'd rather be with him alone while I can.' She'd looked straight at her friend. 'Immie, this isn't going to last. I know that. I'd be a fool not to. But while it does—'

She'd broken off, and to her dismay, Imogen had stared silently at her. Then spoken.

'You've fallen for him, haven't you?' Her voice had been hollow.

Alexa had answered too fast. 'No—'

But Imogen had only shaken her head. 'Oh, hell,' she'd said.

Then she'd given a huge, heavy sigh, and gazed pityingly at her friend.

The pity was back in her voice now, audible down the line. So was a hesitation that was unusual for her. Alexa cut through it.

'Yes, he's getting married. I know.'

The silence on the phone was eloquent.

'The *bastard*!' hissed Imogen. 'The absolute *bastard*!' Then she launched. 'It's on one of those gossip websites! I've only just logged on. There's a huge pic of Carla Crespi, and then one of him, and then it says about how Carla can give up all hope of getting him back now, because he's just about to announce his engagement. And underneath that is the story about who she is—the fiancée of your precious Guy de bloody Rochemont! It's some cousin or other of his. One of the Lorenz lot. They've dug up some pic of her at some *schloss*. She looks like a painted dummy. Daddy's got one of the family banks, so they're keeping all the money in the family—nice and convenient!' Imogen's voice was scathing.

'Yes, well, that's how they've always stayed so rich,' replied Alexa.

There was so much calmness in her voice that it astonished her. Beneath the calm she could feel the information that Imogen was forcing on her pushing into the interstices in her brain. She tried to force it out—she didn't want to know anything about who it was that Guy de Rochemont had chosen to marry—but it was there, vivid in her consciousness. All she could do was ignore it. Turn away from it.

Imogen had cottoned on to another thing now. The fact that Alexa already knew about the engagement.

'So did he deign to tell you?' she demanded. 'Or did you find out the way I did?'

Of course she hadn't found out the way Imogen had! She never looked at such sites, or picked up the kind of magazine that followed the rich and famous in their glamorous lifestyles. Imogen, she knew, even when she'd realised just what was going on between Alexa and Guy de Rochemont, still made a point of being assiduous in her perusal of such sources.

'Believe me, Alexa, if that man is up to stuff you should know about, I'll be on to it!' she'd said, way back. 'I can tell you straight off that it's plain as my face that Carla Crespi is dead set on picking up with him again, for a start.'

But Imogen's vigilance had not been necessary. Nor had Alexa ever thought it would be. For why should Guy conceal anything from her? Let alone the fact that their affair had run its course, as she knew it must one fine day...

'He told me this morning,' she said. The calmness was holding.

There was an intake of breath from Imogen.

Alexa went on, pre-empting any outburst from her friend. 'So, obviously I wished him well, gave him my felicitations, and said goodbye to him. We parted perfectly amicably.'

There was another eloquent silence down the line. Alexa realised that she was gripping the phone hard, yet try as she might she could not make her fingers slacken. Instead, she concentrated on holding that calmness in her voice.

'Imogen, I knew this day would come, and that's that. Now it has. That's all there is to it. There's absolutely no point my making a fuss about it. Guy de Rochemont walked into my life, and now he's walked out of it. End of story. And I'm fine. Absolutely fine. Honestly. Completely fine. *Fine.*'

Again she tried to slacken her grip on the phone, and again for some annoying reason her fingers would not obey her. Something seemed to be gripping her throat as well. Choking her.

At the other end of the line she could hear her name being spoken. Then again. Then, 'I'm coming over,' said

Imogen. And underneath, as she was disconnecting, Alexa heard a sibilant, hissing expletive. '*Bastard*!'

'Guy! *Servus! Wie gehts, wie gehts?*'

The voice greeting him was jovial and welcoming. Guy's arm was taken, and he was all but steered in the direction his host wanted. Guy's jaw tightened. But then that was, after all, exactly what Heinrich von Lorenz *was* doing— steering him in the direction that suited him personally. And suited his damn investment bank. His tottering investment bank, brought to the brink of ruin.

Familiar anger bit within him. Deep and highly masked. Why the *hell* hadn't Heinrich come to him earlier? Why had he bluffed it out for months, getting more and more mired in toxic debt? Pride, that was why, Guy knew. Expensive, unaffordable pride.

Then his anger veered round to target himself. He should have picked up on the depth of the problems Lorenz Investment was having. Dammit, that was his job—taking the helicopter view of everything—*everything!*—that fell within the labyrinthine world of Rochemont-Lorenz. It was the job he'd inherited from his father, and the job he was stuck with.

A caustic glint showed temporarily in his eyes. How many people envied him? Not just those outside the Rochemont-Lorenz behemoth, but even those within. How many considered his position one they would love for themselves? The titular and *de facto* head of a vast, powerful, immensely rich dynasty.

Well, it was nearly ten years since the heavy mantle had fallen on his shoulders, in his early twenties—thanks to the premature death of his father. It was a death to which, Guy knew bitterly, the role he had passed on to his son had contributed in its ceaseless demands on him. Guy was no longer—if he ever had been—a willing occupier of that grandiose position. It might sound good—and, yes, it certainly came with wealth and power, with a social cachet and a historical heritage that lent glamour to the name and role—but it came with a weight of responsibility that exacted its own heavy price.

A price that had suddenly become crippling.

But I have no option but to pay it! No damn option!

His mouth tightened as he went into the ritual of greeting Heinrich and his wife Annelise, in the baronial hall of their Alpine *schloss*. It was Heinrich's residence of choice, for it had once belonged to an archduke and still bore Hapsburg arms above the mantel—arms which, defunct as they were, nevertheless intimated an association with royalty that Heinrich took pleasure in emphasising. The Lorenz quarterings might not have reached further back than a bare century and a half, but Heinrich took inordinate pride in them. Suppressed anger flared again momentarily in Guy. Just as Heinrich took inordinate and clearly unjustified pride in his financial acumen.

Pride goeth before a fall.

The sobering words of the Bible stung Guy's consciousness. Lorenz Investment was as near to falling as if it were a metre away from a precipice. But from the expansiveness of Heinrich's greeting it was impossible to tell how perilously positioned he was. Yet he knew, all right, just how bad things were, despite all his avuncular bonhomie. Again Guy's eyes darkened. He'd taken his eye off the Lorenz Investment balance sheet, targeted his attention at other parts of the operation that had seemed to be in more serious straits courtesy of the global recession, and by the time he'd knocked together the requisite heads, re-set the vulnerable financial thermostats to 'sound' across the multiple divisions and corporations that formed the complex corpus of Rochemont-Lorenz, the window of opportunity for a far less painless rescue package for Lorenz Investment had passed.

And now Heinrich had done what he should have done six months ago, and disclosed the full state of affairs.

And called for the ultimate rescue package.

One that would not just bail out his bank, but achieve his dearest wish…

Had Heinrich been planning this all along? Guy would not have put it past him. He had always known that Heinrich had ambitions to further his branch of the family by any means at his disposal—but Guy had always been uncooperative. Not just for business reasons—Heinrich's mismanagement at Lorenz Investment was proof that had been wise—but for far more cogent reasons. Heinrich's love of royal residences was not the predominant evidence of his fondness for the way royalty did things.

Dynastic marriages were.

For years Guy had simply ignored the subtle and less than subtle comments, insinuations and outright hints. So Heinrich had no sons, only a daughter to inherit his place within Rochemont-Lorenz? So what? This was the twenty-first century. Heinrich might think it impossible, but there was already a sprinkling of highly competent female Rochemonts and Lorenzs taking their place in the higher corporate echelons of the family, and there was no reason why Louisa, if she showed any talent, shouldn't join those ranks in time.

Not that—from what he recalled of Louisa—she seemed to have shown any signs of financial acumen. She was studying something like ecology, he vaguely remembered, and his impression of her was that she was quite shy.

But, shy or not, she should surely be in evidence this evening—as yet, she was not. Guy's brows drew together.

Despite the effusiveness of Heinrich's greeting, and the benign graciousness of Annelise's, Guy had seen the latter's eyes go repeatedly towards the staircase curling around to the upper floors of the *schloss*.

Of Louisa there was conspicuously no sign. Guy's initial reaction on realising she was not there was momentary relief, but as the minutes wore on, and he was subjected to the kind of irrelevant and time-filling social conversation on the part of his hosts that he found as hypocritical as it was irksome, he could feel irritation piercing through the predominant emotion of anger at Heinrich's machinations and the unacceptable fall-out from his incompetence. He could see Heinrich and Annelise getting tenser about their daughter's continuing absence even while they were determinedly not mentioning it.

Impatiently, Guy decided to cut through the flam. 'Where is Louisa?'

His blunt question brought an instant prevaricatory response, which only irritated him further.

'You must make allowances,' added Annelise in a saccharine voice. 'Of course she is anxious to make the very highest impression on you, Guy, knowing how demanding your taste in the fairer sex is. She is bound to want to look her very best for you. Your reputation is quite formidable, as you must well know. Ah, look—' the relief was plain in her voice as her eyes went to the staircase, '—here she is now!'

Guy turned. Descending the staircase was Louisa.

His intended bride.

And anyone looking less like the prospective Madame Guy de Rochemont it would have been hard to find.

For a moment, as vivid as a splash of scarlet in a monochrome photo, another image imposed itself—elegant, soignée, *superbe*…

He thrust it away. He had done with it now.

At his side, he heard Louisa's mother give a click of exasperation and dismay. And he could see why. Her daughter had clearly made no effort whatsoever for the occasion. She was wearing jeans, a jumper and trainers, her hair was in a ponytail and her face was bereft of make-up.

'Louisa, what are you *thinking* of?' demanded her mother.

Her father had gone red—a mix of chagrin and anger.

Wariness flared in the wide brown eyes as Louisa approached. 'I didn't have time to change,' she answered. 'And what's the point, anyway? I've known Guy for ever. He knows what he's getting.'

There was a flicker of defiance in her question, and Guy felt himself in sympathy. Louisa's preference for casual style might not fit with what he himself preferred, or what the world would expect of his wife—every eye would be pitilessly upon her—but that was not her fault any more than her father's ambitions for his daughter were—or the mess Heinrich had made of his bank.

Guy's frustration worsened. If there had been any way—any at all—of calling Heinrich's infernal bluff, he would have done so. But the damnable thing was that the man was right. Any visible sign of a bail-out—internal or otherwise—of Lorenz Investment would, at this delicate stage in consolidating Rochemont-Lorenz against the recession, send danger signals ricocheting around and beyond the confines of the dynasty. The potentially disastrous consequences could, at worst, have a domino effect, taking down a lot more than Heinrich's bank. With sufficient time Guy knew he could nail any potential danger, ring-fencing Lorenz Investment, but time was not what he or the bank had. Which was why Heinrich—damn him!—had argued the case for this archaic and Machiavellian dynastic solution.

'My dear boy…' It was a form of address that had set Guy's teeth on edge when Heinrich had disclosed his master plan for not just saving his bank and his own skin, but achieving personal advancement within the clan. 'It is the perfect solution! A union between our two branches provides the perfect occasion for closer financial ties— what could be more reasonable? There will be no occasion for press speculation or undue attention from the financial analysts. Any financial…adjustment—' his choice of ano-dyne term for *bail-out* had further angered Guy, already feeling the edges of a man trap closing around him '—can be made entirely painlessly,' Heinrich had concluded breez-ily, blithely skipping over the punishing financial cost of what it would take to protect Lorenz Investment against its toxic debts, incurred solely because of Heinrich's rash and greedy strategy for over-expansion.

He had provided in an unwise coda. 'Why, a hundred years ago such an…investment—' now he was present-ing the bail-out as a commercial opportunity, Guy had thought viciously '—would have been regarded as a fitting bride-price! Cemented, of course—' he'd smiled with bland optimism at his prospective son-in-law '—with a position at your right hand on the senior global executive board.'

Guy's answer had been short and to the point.

'This is a salvage operation, Heinrich. Nothing more. And be aware, *very* aware, that I undertake it solely for the good of us all. This debacle is of your making—survival is your only reward.'

Heinrich had bridled, then changed umbrage to bon-homie.

'And yours, my boy, is my daughter. It's an ideal match!'

His words had rung hollow, and now, as Guy's gaze rested on Louisa, their echo rang even more hollow. Louisa was a pretty girl, and the casual outfit suited her brunette, gamine looks, but Guy knew with a sharpening of the knife that had been stuck between his ribs by Heinrich that they were not the looks *he* sought in a woman.

The image he had banned from his mind because it belonged to the past, not the future, tried to gain entry. Once more he thrust it aside. Alexa had been an affair, nothing more, he reminded himself brutally—that was all he must remember about her.

Now, like it or not, he had to come to terms with what his future was going to be. A future with Louisa von Lorenz in it. She was standing there, her unvarnished appearance making her look more suited to being a chalet girl than chatelaine of a hundred-room *schloss*.

Louisa's father barrelled forward, seizing her arm. 'Get back upstairs and get changed immediately!' he hissed at his wayward daughter.

Guy stepped forward.

'Quite unnecessary,' he said. 'Louisa—'

His eye contact with her was veiled, concealing his simmering frustration. He did not want to take it out on the hapless Louisa. Then he turned back to Annelise.

'Shall we go in to dinner?' his hostess said brightly, clearly wanting to move the evening on.

Wordlessly, Guy slipped his hand beneath Louisa's woolen-clad elbow to lead her forward towards the vast panelled dining room beyond.

With iron self-control, he tamped down the dark, bitter emotions scything through him.

CHAPTER FOUR

ALEXA was painting. Painting and painting and painting. She'd been painting all week. A new commission had arrived, and she had gone into overdrive. Imogen had lined up at least two more portraits, and Alexa was thankful, knowing that her friend had done it deliberately. So far she'd managed to hold herself together, though when Imogen had come round that first evening she'd come very close to cracking. Imogen had urged her on—but Alexa would not oblige her. Would not even let her call Guy a bastard. Let alone allow her to give all the details about his forthcoming marriage.

'You should *know*!' Imogen had wailed.

But Alexa had only said, 'What for?' and refused to let her friend say more.

Even so, it had been impossible to silence her completely.

'According to the internet and the press, quoting the girl's mother, this Lorenz cousin has been groomed to marry Guy de Rochemont for *ever*! There was a really yukky bit about how the daughter had been brought up to take her place at the head of the whole damn dynasty. Like they were royalty or something!'

'Well, there *are* some titles washing around,' Alexa had pointed out, keeping her answer reasonable—for being reasonable was essential. So was being composed. And calm. Very calm. 'And obviously there is the *"de"* and the *"von"* in the names. So they are clearly aristocracy in that sense.'

'Inbred, too!' Imogen had muttered darkly.

Alexa had not responded. Her consciousness had been filled with a memory of Guy, walking out of the shower, his honed, water-beaded torso as perfectly planed as his face. 'Inbred' was *not* a word to describe him…

Then, something Imogen had said snapped her mind back.

'…their only daughter—just turned nineteen…'

'What?' She stared at Imogen. 'What did you just say?'

Imogen nodded, glad she had finally pricked Alexa's calmness. She thought Alexa should be spitting with rage against Guy for having so unceremoniously dumped her. 'Yup, his precious family bride is only nineteen!'

Alexa had paled, shocked by the disclosure. 'She can't be! Guy's in his thirties. She'd be almost fourteen years younger than him. Nearly a whole generation!'

Imogen smiled nastily. 'So, cradle-snatcher as well, then—plus complete bastard!'

Alexa flinched. 'Immie, don't. Please.' Then she plunged on, 'But I can't, *can't* believe he'd marry someone that young.'

'He'll probably enjoy a young wife. Someone naive and easy to manipulate. Someone he can impress. Make a fool of.' She cast a dark look at Alexa. 'Though you don't have to be nineteen to be taken for a ride by Guy de Rochemont!'

But Alexa was still too shocked to react to the jibe. 'She can't be only nineteen,' she echoed.

'Well, she is. And don't tell me he won't find it convenient. He'll be able to pocket her dowry—Daddy's bank!—to add to his collection, and then after a night deflowering her he can set up a sophisticated, grown-up mistress—like you were, Alexa, whether or not you like that word—and sow his oats with *her*, not some inexperienced little teenage virgin!'

Alexa's lips pressed together. 'Immie, don't. That's a completely unwarranted accusation! Guy would never do that! Be unfaithful to his wife.'

Imogen laughed harshly. 'Oh yeah? Wanna bet? Honestly, Alexa, you're as naive about him as if it was *you* who was nineteen!' She glared at her friend. 'You just don't get it, do you? Face the truth, Alexa—Guy de Rochemont *used* you! He treated you appallingly. It's unbelievable. He turned up whenever he wanted and there you were, waiting and willing. Or if he decided he could fit you into his oh-so-busy schedule, he had you flown out to him—like some whore!' Her voice sharpened, her expression fierce. 'He used you for on-demand sex, Alexa!'

'No!' Alexa's denial was automatic, instant.

'*Yes,*' insisted Imogen.

Alexa shut her eyes, twisting her head away. Imogen's ugly words seared into her brain. *No!* she wanted to cry out again. *It wasn't like that! It wasn't!*

Denial fought with doubt.

Imogen hammered home her condemnation.

'Guy treated you like dirt—why shouldn't he treat his wife like dirt too?'

'Stop it—I won't let you say such things about him!' protested Alexa, clinging to denial. 'You don't know him, Immie. I do.'

Imogen looked at her. '*Do* you?' she said.

Alexa closed her eyes. Inside her lids, a thousand images and memories replayed themselves.

Then, 'Yes, I do,' she said, as she opened them again and let her gaze rest unflinchingly on her condemning friend. 'Guy is not like that. I know. I know you didn't like the way he came and went, but I'll tell you, and I'll tell you again and go on telling you, I was OK with it. It suited us both.'

Imogen just nodded. 'Right. So will it suit you when he swans back into your life and suggests picking up again where you left off, because his honeymoon's over?'

For a moment as brief as the stab of a knife emotion leapt in Alexa's throat. Then, very carefully, she answered.

'That isn't Guy. Whatever the reasons he's marrying— and for all I know he's loved her for years and has been waiting for her to grow up—' She ignored the derisive snort from Imogen at this fairy-tale explanation. 'He'll treat her honourably. Why shouldn't he?'

Imogen just looked at her. 'Because,' she spelt out, 'he didn't treat *you* "honourably", that's why. And, Alexa, you're no Carla Crespi—she's as hard as nails and must have *ambition* written all the way through her like a stick of rock. So what excuse was there for the way he treated you? Apart from the excuse *you* keep coming up with? Saying you *liked* being treated like that! OK, OK, I won't go on about it any more—I'll just leave you to find out the truth for yourself. Because I'll bet you, hand on heart, that that painted little doll he's marrying won't keep him between her sheets. I will bet you the sum of one hundred pounds—cash down, Alexa—that he'll be running to another woman, wedding ring on his finger or not!'

'You're wrong,' said Alexa. Her teeth were gritted, her throat tight.

But Imogen had only levelled her remorseless gaze on her. 'One hundred pounds. On the table. And I,' she said, 'am going to win it.'

* * *

Hairpin bends snaked along the mountain side, heading towards the pass into Switzerland, away from the ducal *schloss* and his future bride. Guy drove fast and furiously, the powerful engine of his low, lean car eating up the curves along with the miles. The concentration it required to negotiate the precipitous Alpine road was a welcome— necessary!—diversion for his mind.

How the hell had he ended up in such a damnable situation?

But the question was pointless. Rhetorical. He knew very well how—had played it out a thousand times in his head. It didn't matter how he cut it, marrying Heinrich's daughter was the safest way to protect Rochemont-Lorenz. And protecting Rochemont-Lorenz was his job. His purpose. Just as it had been *his* father's and his father's before him, for over two hundred years. The weight of dynasty, destiny, pressed down upon him.

As he climbed the pass his eyes were bleak. It was nothing new, carrying such a weight. And for some it had been far worse than his burden. Only two generations ago his great-great-uncle Lorenz had liquidated his assets a week before the Anschluss of Germany with Austria, banking the remainder in a Swiss vault rather than let the Nazis sequester it. The gesture hadn't gone unpunished, and his great-great-aunt had become a widow, her husband 'disappeared' into Nazi prison camps.

Her sister-in-law had divorced the husband she'd loved to marry one of Hitler's top cronies, who'd fancied such a prestigious wife, in order to halt any further 'disappearances' in her branch of the family—and to preserve what she could of the Polish branch of the bank, first from Nazi and then Communist despoilation.

After the war another cousin had courted Stalin, funding Russian industry despite his father-in-law being despatched to the gulags for being a 'dissident intellectual' with his academic work suppressed. Even in less drastic times personal fulfilment had always been put aside for the sake of what was best for Rochemont-Lorenz.

His own father had wanted to be a professional sportsman—but what use would an Olympic rower have been to the family? So he'd become a banker instead—steering the family fortunes through the EC corridors of Brussels and Strasbourg and the opening up of the former Eastern bloc, and marrying a woman he did not love because it was a match that profited the family, whose perpetual requirements outweighed the petty emotions of individual members. Petty, transient emotions, that would not last if they were starved sufficiently, denied sufficiently.

Emotions as petty as desire. And more than desire…

That waterfall of pale hair, the slender, graceful body, the porcelain skin, and those grey, luminous eyes widening in wonder as the moment came upon her…

Guy's hand gripped the gear lever, shifting up to match the engine speed. What use to think of such things? To remember a time when he'd been free—free to have Alexa in his life? That was in the past. In the future was following in his parents' footsteps. Doing as they had done. He took another hairpin, faster than he should, as though by driving fast he could escape the inescapable, and thought about his parents' marriage. Neither had loved the other, but they had married all the same, and made a pretty good job of it along the way. Respect and consideration went a long way in a marriage.

Would it do the same for his?

The question hung in the high mountain air.

And found no answer.

Only as he glanced upwards, seeing an eagle soaring on

thermals, came the sure and certain knowledge that such freedom as the eagle had would never be his again.

Ahead of him, the dark mouth of the road tunnel started to open, swallowing all that entered. He depressed the accelerator and let himself be swallowed up.

'It's good that she is so young.' The voice speaking was beautifully modulated, and it was impossible to tell from it what its owner thought—other than the words expressed.

'Too young.' Guy's answer showed all too clearly his disquiet.

His mother paused momentarily in her needlework. Outside on the parterre an autumn leaf eddied intermittently. The sky was grey above the Loire château, but there was still light in the air, and the ornamental trees marching along the boundary of this section of the gardens still held their leaves, despite the season. Along the gravel, a peacock strolled disconsolately, his tail furled.

'It's an advantage,' Claudine de Rochemont said. 'It will make her impressionable to your charms. It would be good for her, Guy, if she fell in love with you. It would not be hard for you to make that happen, you know.' Green eyes, so similar to her son's, rested on him.

Her son frowned. 'God, no!' he exclaimed feelingly. 'How could you hope for such a thing? Unrequited love is the very last thing I would want for her! None of this mess is of her making, and I certainly acquit her of any ambition to marry me.' He gave a short, humourless laugh. 'Her appearance at dinner was enough to convince me of that. She had no design to attract me. She had neglected to change out of her jeans—Heinrich and Annelise were not pleased.'

'No, I imagine they would not be,' observed his mother. 'But Louisa is very pretty, Guy—Annelise took pains to send me the studio shots she had done in the summer. Too overdone, but that's just Annelise's taste. Underneath the bones are good.'

'Pretty?' echoed Guy condemningly, and said no more.

He did not want 'pretty'. His eyes veiled, masking memories.

His mother glanced at him assessingly. 'Not all women can aspire to the allure of Signorina Crespi,' she remarked dryly.

Guy gave a slight shrug but said nothing, aware that his mother was still looking at him. He glanced at his watch. He wanted out of this conversation, but knew he owed his mother the courtesy of letting her raise the subject. He could hardly exclude her.

'So, what are the plans in respect of the wedding?'

He glanced back up at her. 'I have no idea. It is not imminent.' His lips pressed tightly. 'Despite Heinrich's eagerness!'

His mother nodded. 'That is sensible. Such affairs should not be rushed. I must get in touch with Annelise. And of course Louisa must visit here too.'

'I suppose so,' said Guy heavily. He glanced at his watch again. 'Maman, you must excuse me. I have a dinner engagement in Paris. The helicopter is on standby.'

Again that speculative look was in his mother's eyes. 'A personal engagement?' she ventured.

Guy's expression closed. 'No. Business.' He paused, then said deliberately, 'I know enough, Maman, to follow the conventions! The only press coverage about me outside the financial press will be in respect of Louisa. And now, forgive me, I must go.'

He took his leave, dutifully kissing his mother on her scented cheek, and strode off. From her place on the Louis

Quinze sofa his mother watched him go. Her expression was troubled. A long engagement for a man like her son, fêted by women and used to their enjoyment, was not a good idea. Louisa von Lorenz *was* young—but a pretty, adoring young bride, swept off her feet by a handsome, sophisticated and experienced husband, could make a workable marriage. And who knew? A softening look in her eyes. Perhaps an adoring young bride would finally inspire her son to do what would be best for him—fall in love.

She picked up her needlework again, the troubled look gone, replaced by hope. Above all she wished her son the gift of a marriage based on love. Even if it took a *marriage de covenance* to achieve it, as it had in her case.

Would it be so for her son as well?

For now, she could only watch, and wait, in hope.

CHAPTER FIVE

'ALEXA, it's the best thing that could have happened to you. Richard Saxonby is seriously nice. Plus he's good-looking, well-heeled, and really keen on you. You couldn't do better!'

Imogen's encomium was a ringing endorsement of what Alexa already knew about the man who was asking her out. Richard was indeed seriously nice. Plus he was good company and intelligent, which was important to her—though Alexa did not regard as highly as Imogen his financial status and keenness on her. She liked him, and, yes, with her eyes she could see he was good looking, with his brown hair and brown eyes, and sturdy, muscular build.

But did that mean she should go out with him?

'Yes!' urged Imogen. 'You can't go on moping for ever!'

'I am not moping,' Alexa replied evenly.

'Just living like a nun.' Imogen said acidly. She rolled her eyes. 'It's been four months since Guy de Rochemont did the dirty on you. And since then—' she ignored the customary rejection Alexa always gave whenever she heard Guy criticised '—all you've done is work, work, work. If it hadn't been for me plaguing you, you wouldn't have seen a soul except your clients! C'mon, Alexa—it's time to rejoin the female race. Guy's history—and you're well out of it.

Find someone normal, with emotions, not just some jerk who thinks his zillions entitle him to treat women like disposable sex toys whenever he wants some personal R&R when he's not adding to his gold piles. That's why Richard Saxonby's so good—he's *nice*, for Pete's sake!'

'Too nice,' Alexa prevaricated. 'I don't want to—'

She stopped. Saying more would be revealing, and since Imogen was only too ready to find any reason to persist in her castigation of Guy de Rochemont Alexa did not want to add any fuel to the fire. But silently she completed the sentence in her own head.

I don't want to give him false hope...

Even as the words formed she felt the familiar scrape against her heart. If only familiarity lessened the pain—but it had never yet seemed to. For over four months her strategy had simply been to ignore the pain. Acknowledge it was there, but otherwise ignore it. After all, what else could she do? She had fallen in love—stupidly and unintentionally and rashly—with a man who was the very last she should have fallen in love with. He'd never expected her to, and if he'd known she had he would have been appalled with her. It wasn't his fault she'd gone and done it, which meant that the fall-out was hers and hers alone. She had to tough it out, that was all, because what else was there to do? At some point, surely, she would wake up one morning and realise that she was over him? Then, and only then, would she be ready to do what Imogen was vocally urging her to do—move on.

Move on to another man.

But that was the stumbling block. It was unimaginable still even to *think* of becoming emotionally involved with another man. The very thought was impossible. And for that reason she didn't want anyone becoming emotionally hung up on her. Especially not someone as nice as Richard Saxonby.

She'd met him at one of Imogen's frequent dinner parties, to one of which she'd finally been lured, and it was blatantly obvious he'd been carefully selected as a dinner guest by Imogen, purely to dangle in front of her. She'd been placed next to him, and Alexa had to allow that Richard ticked a lot of boxes. He was nice, funny, good-natured and good-looking.

But he wasn't Guy de Rochemont.

No one is! No one possibly could be!

Alexa laid into her own futile objection ruthlessly. No one was ever going to be Guy, and Guy was beyond her now—beyond her for ever. Her future lay without him, and nothing on earth could change that.

I have to get over him! I have to!

The pain still scraped away at her heart, familiar and futile. So damn, *damn* futile…

And Immie was right. Until she made a determined effort to remake the rest of her life she would inevitably go on 'moping', as her friend so cruelly described her decision to withdraw from the social world, turn in on herself, try and tough it out.

I have to get over him—I have no alternative.

A deep breath filled her lungs, and she lifted her chin. 'All right,' she said, 'I'll give Richard a go.'

Immie shut her eyes. 'At last. Thank God,' she said fervently. Then, less audibly but yet more fervently, she muttered, 'And maybe that bastard who treated you like dirt will finally get the hell out of your head! And stay out!'

Guy was meeting and greeting. As the customary social phrases flowed smoothly from his lips, so familiar to him that he could say them on automatic, his conscious mind was busy. Busy exerting what had become bleakly familiar to him over the last four months—iron self-control over his emotions.

Self-control had been an essential weapon in his personal armoury just about all his life, he recognised. It was what enabled him to function, and always had. It was as necessary as breathing. It enabled him to run the behemoth of Rochemont-Lorenz, bear the mantle that was his by inheritance, and cope with all the endless demands made on him—not only of ensuring that Rochemont-Lorenz would continue to survive and prosper in this uncertain new century but also far more tedious to endure, of being endlessly on call to just about every member of the entire damn clan.

So many relatives! So many gatherings of relatives! *Dieu*, he could have filled his days simply circulating around Europe, and further afield, on a non-stop diet of family social occasions from birthdays to weddings to christenings to funerals. His attendance was expected, his presence courted, and offence taken if he made too many repeated omissions. Ambitions were raised if he decided that relatives active in the myriad companies and enterprises within Rochmont-Lorenz were worth promoting, chagrin taken by those he did not consider sufficiently able.

Not to mention tracking and mitigating the endless politicking and jostling between the different branches—internecine rivalries and alliances alike. Not everyone had been of the opinion that a man in his early twenties—even though he was the son of the oldest branch of the family—should take over the helm from his father at so young an age. There had been plenty of older cousins who had challenged his succession. But Guy's dedication to his role, his cool head and formidable financial acumen, had proved him his father's son both in ability and determination, and now his place at the head of the dynasty was assured—taken for granted, even.

The bleakness in his face was visible momentarily. Just as it was taken for granted that he would continue to guard the fortunes of Rochemont-Lorenz, whatever that required.

Right to the very point of marrying for that purpose.

His eyes glanced sideways.

Louisa was standing beside him—conspicuously so—standing very still as the mill of people in the ballroom ebbed and flowed, and the cluster that Guy was meeting and greeting came and went. She looked ill at ease, saying little, and although Guy made allowances for her youth and inexperience at such formal gatherings, and had sought to reassure her that he would give her all the support he could, that did not mean she would not have to learn how to handle them with the assurance that would be necessary as his wife.

It did not help that she was clearly of marked interest to anyone who knew him, for this was her first appearance in London as his fiancée, and for once her parents were not here. Guy had finally succeeded in shaking them off for his visit here, and Louisa was staying with the family of an old college friend for a weekend in England. Guy would have preferred her not to be here at all—not to be putting her through what was clearly an ordeal for her—but on the other hand she had to get used to the life she would be leading once she was married to him: the endless round of socialising and hostessing. That would best be done without her parents endlessly hovering over her—and over him.

The bleakness flared in his eyes again, mingled with the other emotion that was his constant companion—an emotion that required every ounce of will to control. An emotion that being in London had brought dangerously to the fore. He hadn't been here in four months, and he was glad of it. It only reminded him of what he'd had to do without. Into his mind's eye flicked the image of the eagle soaring, free and unfettered, over the lofty Alpine peaks as he'd headed into the confines of the tunnel. Resentment bit into him at what he was no longer free to do. And what he had to do instead.

At his side, Louisa hesitantly echoed his greeting of whoever it was whose hand he'd just shaken. His glance went sideways again. His mouth tightened. Annelise might not be here in person, but she was here in spirit, given the choice of gown for her daughter tonight. The dress was far too overpowering, stiff and grandiose. Presumably Annelise had been intending to make Louisa look older, more sophisticated. Instead it just emphasised her youth— and her evident awkwardness.

She'd looked a whole lot better in the jeans she'd worn that first evening—casual teenage wear, Guy thought. Since then, whenever he'd set eyes on her, she'd always been wearing outfits obviously chosen by her mother, and never to her advantage. He'd made no comment, not wanting to make her even more unsure of herself, but had made a mental note to ensure that as soon as they were married he would put her in the hands of someone who knew how to dress her properly, to bring out the best in her.

Memory stung like an unwelcome wasp.

His murmured accolade—*superbe…*

The image was vivid in his mind.

A slender column of burnt sienna raw silk, sleeveless and high-necked, exposing graceful arms and accentuating the subtle curves of breast and hip…

His mouth tightened even more. Why was he remembering Alexa when she was gone from his life now? His future lay with Louisa and he must remember that, must banish distracting memories of his lost freedom.

At his side, Louisa's gaze suddenly flickered up to his, and he saw anxiety flare briefly. He curved a smile to his mouth to reassure her, and hoped he'd succeeded. As he'd said to his mother, none of this was her fault. A frown drew his eyebrows together. Despite the punishing demands of starting to sort out Lorenz Investment on top of all his other concerns, he'd made an effort to spend what time he could with Louisa, seeking to get to know her and, above all, establish that she was prepared to enter into such a marriage with him.

Like his parents, hers, too, had married for the sake of Rochemont-Lorenz, and he was as reassured as he could be in the circumstances that Louisa was willing to marry him, and that she understood that for now his first concern must be saving her father's bank. Once that was secure he would give Louisa the attention she deserved, get to know her better and draw her out of her shyness and reticence.

A young, adoring bride. His eyes frowned. Was that what he wanted? Even as the thought came, he knew the answer.

No.

But perhaps for Louisa—who, like him, had not sought this marriage—it would be the best way for her to find happiness.

The frown turned to bleakness. For him, happiness seemed unlikely.

Once more his eyes chilled. Once more his iron self-control hammered down—familiar and exacting. And absolutely essential.

* * *

'More champagne?'

Alexa gave a slight shake of her head. 'Not for the moment. I'm doing fine.'

She was, too—and not just in consuming the champagne that was circulating generously at this crowded charity gala. She was doing fine just being out for the evening with Richard. As fine as could be expected. She'd had cold feet half a dozen times since she'd given in to Imogen, but each time she'd gone through the same dogged loop of facing up to the unalterable truth that she simply could not go on living like a hermit for the rest of her existence. She had to get on with her life.

Even so, when Richard had disclosed that he was inviting her to be his partner at this charity gala, she had almost backed out. Something more low-key would have been preferable for a first evening. On the other hand as she'd gone on to consider, a charity gala was preferable to some kind of quiet, intimate *tête-à-tête* over dinner. Nevertheless, it had taken a stern degree of resolution to get herself ready for this evening and come here on Richard's arm.

Although he could not be faulted as an evening companion, she knew she was far from relaxed. The commercial property company where he was a consultant architect was supporting this event. At his table was a mix of fellow architects and their partners, and she was conscious of being reserved—even for her. Conscious, too, of the presence of so many glitteringly arrayed guests—the charity had clearly captured a good number of London's seriously wealthy people. The realisation made her uneasy. Evoked memories and associations she did not want. She felt the familiar scrape across her heart.

But the last thing she wanted was to spoil Richard's evening by being anything other than a good guest, and so, despite her reserve, she entered into the general conversation at the table. As the evening wore on, a sobering truth came to her. Had she not ever gone through that rash, misguided affair with Guy de Rochemont—or rather, she amended, had she not committed the folly of allowing herself to so stupidly fall in love with him—she would have enjoyed Richard Saxonby's attentions far more.

It makes such sense to fall for him...

Surely, with time, she could make herself do so? Surely, with time, she could start to feel for him, finally expunge the hopeless, dead-end love she'd felt for Guy that was keeping her in this pointless limbo? Surely, she thought, as she smiled pleasantly at Richard, accepting his invitation to dance as the dinner, speeches and charity auction finally gave way to a general mingling around the huge room, surely it would not be too hard to take pleasure in lifting her eyes to his, letting their warmth set a glow in hers, letting his well-made mouth kiss hers? It should not be too hard to come to desire him. To fall—one day, when the time was right and they had come to know each other and desire each other—in love with him?

Then the music ended, and the couples on the floor relinquished each other and started to disperse back to their tables. Across the wide expanse of the room, as Richard let go of her and she started to head to her seat again, the pattern of people shifted and her eyes went through a newly opened gap, far across the ballroom. She stopped absolutely, totally still.

And knew that never in a hundred years could she fall in love with Richard or any other man.

Because the man she still loved was looking straight at her.

It was Alexa.

For a moment Guy's line of sight encompassed only

her—a tall, slender column of wine-rich burgundy—then it widened to take in her arm, resting on the sleeve of one of the many tuxedos, and the wearer of the tuxedo looking proprietorially down at her.

Instinctively Guy moved forward. It took only moments, and Alexa hadn't moved. Only her expression had changed. The initial flare of shock in her eyes as they had lighted on him was now veiled, and she seemed to wait, immobile, for his approach across the floor of the ballroom.

'Good evening, Alexa.'

His voice was smooth, the accent, as ever, hardly noticeable.

Unlike the rest of him.

Her eyes, beneath their veil, were sucked to him. In her limbs she felt a sudden debilitating weakness, as if they might not hold her upright. But she must force them to. Must force herself not, *not* to let her eyes feed on that tall, effortlessly elegant figure that instantly, immediately, made every other man in the room look clumsy and lumpish. She must *not* feast on the fabulous planes of his face, the sable feathering of his hair, and *not*, above all, drown unstoppably in those deep green eyes that were resting on her and making her feel dizzy, weightless, breathless.

Oh, dear God, let this not be happening…

She could hear the call in her head, hear all the sense that she was possessed of decrying what was happening, what she was doing, and her fatal reaction. She was totally unprepared for this, her guard helplessly, hopelessly absent, so that there was nothing she could do except reel from the impact of his presence.

Another cry sounded in her head, coming from deeper yet.

It shouldn't be like this!

She shouldn't be so overcome like this. She shouldn't!

She'd had four months—four whole months to come to terms with the end of the affair. Four months to build up that vital, essential distance from what had been to what her life now had to be. Four months to do without Guy de Rochemont in her life. To get him out of her head.

And it took a single moment now to make her realise that all her efforts to get over him had been utterly in vain.

Dismay drenched through her, mingling with the emotion that had seized her throat, her lungs, as she'd recognised him—that was still seizing her now, making it impossible for her to speak, impossible to do what she must, which was simply to say his name, in a calm, level voice, suitable for the occasion, in acknowledgment of his greeting. Then they would exchange pleasantries, he would wish her well, and stroll away again. Back to his life. Back to his world. Back to the woman he was going to marry.

That was what she must do.

But there was nothing. She could not speak.

Then, like a knight to her rescue, Richard was speaking. Prompting her.

'Alexa?'

There was nothing in his voice but appropriate social enquiry, but thankfully it served to catalyse her into responding. A quick smile parted her lips.

'Richard—this is Guy de Rochemont. I had the privilege of painting his portrait a while ago.'

A glint showed in the green eyes. 'The privilege was mine, Alexa.' He paused minutely. 'I did not think you would be here this evening…' There was the slightest Gallic intonation in the comment, so that it sounded like no more than a passing remark.

She made herself give her quick smile again.

'Nor I,' she said. She glanced at Richard, encompassing him in her reply. 'Richard was kind enough to invite me.'

Her escort smiled acknowledgement. Without noticing it, Alexa leant slightly towards him. There was a flicker of enquiry on Guy's expression. Richard held out his hand.

'Richard Saxonby—Guy de Rochemont,' she said, her voice and manner relaxed.

Guy took the outstretched hand, which was firm and solid. Like the man. Good-looking, too, he acknowledged, with intelligent eyes and a face that found it easy to smile. Personable. Attractive. He could see why Alexa was with him. There was nothing to dislike in this Richard Saxonby.

Which made it illogical, therefore, that he should have a sudden impulse, ruthlessly controlled, to wrest Alexa's hand from the man's sleeve, clamp it in his own grip, and walk off with her.

Walk off with her, pile her into a car, take her back to her apartment, his hotel—any damn place, providing it had a bed in it and no Richard Saxonby or any other damn male!—and then strip Alexa of that utterly unnecessary evening dress, loosen the clips on her hair to let its pale waterfall cascade like silk over her shoulders, cover her opening mouth with his and get her beautiful naked body to himself. Completely, luxuriously, satiatingly to himself.

His jaw tightened, and he slammed down on his overpowering impulse. That wasn't going to happen. Despite the flash of desire momentarily possessing him, Alexa Harcourt was in the past. Everything to do with her was in the past. He'd made his decision, terminated their relationship. So if she wanted to have a relationship with another man, such as this Richard Saxonby, what was it to him? Nothing. *Rien de tout.*

The familiar sense of self-control settled over him, shutting out everything that had to be shut out, kept down. Smoothly he exchanged the socially required introductions with the man who was now clearly enjoying Alexa's beautiful body—an enjoyment which was nothing to do with Guy any more, nor would be ever again, and therefore something about which he was unconcerned. Any other reaction was inappropriate to the circumstances. He no longer had Alexa for himself—a decision which had been his and his alone—and therefore if she wished, as *evidemment* she did wish, to bestow herself upon this man—any other man, in fact—it was of no moment to him at all. None.

And, because it was so, all that was required now was to do as he proceeded to do: loose the man's hand and give an acknowledging nod of his head towards Alexa. He ignored the fact that her shoulder was brushing that of this Richard Saxonby, with his good-looking face and well-made body and his air of masculine assurance—and why not? He had Alexa in his bed—a presence which would make any man satisfied. With a brief indentation of his mouth in farewell, Guy took his leave and walked away from her and her bed-partner of choice these days, and returned to his own party.

It had been the work of a few moments only—a fleeting episode in an evening which was like a thousand other evenings in his life spent at some social gathering in which he had no particular interest, but where his attendance was expected and therefore was provided. He had not even had to take regard, for those few brief, inconsequential moments, of his fiancée and her *gaucherie* at this first social outing at his side. For, just before his glancing gaze had lighted on the unexpected sight of Alexa Harcourt, Louisa had murmured her excuses and slipped away to what he assumed was the ladies' room.

She had still not returned, but he did not begrudge her her respite—indeed, he found himself glad she had not witnessed his exchange with Alexa. Not that it was any concern of his fiancée, or anyone else. Although he had never drawn attention to Alexa's role in his life, it would have been more marked had he *not* acknowledged the presence that evening of the woman whom he had commissioned to make his likeness in oils. He had no wish for Louisa to be in a social situation of any kind with any female who had occupied a place in his life that she, as his fiancée and then wife, would never occupy. They were orbits that would never meet, never intersect.

As he resumed the party, slipping back into the banal chit-chat of his company, for a few brief moments in his mind's eye he saw that eagle again, soaring away over the peaks, far, far beyond. Ahead of him opened the tunnel, leading into the mountain's stony depths.

'Richard, would you excuse me a moment?'

Alexa's voice was steady, her manner just as it had been five minutes earlier.

But only on the outside. On the inside her nerves were jangling as if a current had been set through them. She had to get away.

Hardly waiting for his acknowledgement of her intention, she turned away, threading through the throng towards the blessed respite of the ladies' room. There was a sickness in her insides, and her throat was tight. The moment she was in the Ladies she plunged into a stall, shutting fast the door and clinging to it. How long she was in there she didn't know—knew only that her heart was pounding, her mind ragged. Gradually, very gradually, the shock—more than shock—of seeing Guy again started to recede. With intense effort she forced herself to calm the hectic beating of her heart, banned herself from letting the scene replay in her head. It didn't matter—it didn't matter a jot that she had seen Guy again! She would not *let* it matter!

She dared not…

She took the deep breath, steadying herself. Then, unlocking the door, she stepped out of the stall. Running on automatic, she crossed to the washbasins and mechanically started to wash her hands. As she did so, she noticed a large, opulent ring, with a glittering stone inset, on the surrounding vanity unit. There was no other person present— not even an attendant. Alexa glanced around. It was not the kind of ring to be left lying there. The area was deserted, but just as she was wondering what she should best do, reluctant to pick the ring up in case she might open herself to accusations of theft, there was a bustle behind her and a little cry of relief.

'*Gott seie Danke!*'

Alexa turned to see a young woman dive on the ring and jam it back on her finger. As she did so, Alexa could not but help catch her eye.

'I'm not used to wearing it,' the girl said by way of explanation.

There was a slight Germanic cast to her accent. She smiled at Alexa, who found herself answering with a smile as well as she reached for one of the stash of folded linen towels by the basin.

'I'm glad you remembered it,' she remarked. 'I was wondering who I ought to alert that it was here. It's not the sort of ring one would want to lose.'

The girl made a face. 'I would have got into such trouble,' she said. 'It's some kind of heirloom. Every bride for a million years has had it!' She didn't sound very impressed by the fact, and as she examined it on her finger she didn't look very impressed by the ring either, despite the vast size of the diamonds in the opulent setting.

'It's a magnificent ring,' said Alexa politely.

The girl grimaced. She was pretty, a dusky brunette,

but the gown she was wearing was too overpowering for her, Alexa thought critically. It was in a very stiff lemon silk, with a sweeping panelled skirt and a tight bodice that seemed to crush the girl's breasts.

'It doesn't suit me,' the girl said flatly, still eyeing the ring.

'Well, perhaps you need only wear it for formal occasions,' Alexa answered tactfully. 'Maybe you could ask your fiancé for something simpler, more to your taste, for everyday wear.' Judging by the vastness of the gems, providing a second engagement ring for casual wear would not be a problem for what was evidently a very wealthy fiancé.

The girl's expression changed. 'No, he wouldn't do that. I have to be formal all the time.' She looked down at her dress. 'Like this dress. It doesn't suit me either.'

Alexa frowned slightly. It seemed a shame that the girl couldn't choose a gown she liked. Something in a more youthful style, in a softer material.

'*Your* gown's beautiful!' the girl said impulsively. Then she grimaced again. 'But that wouldn't suit me either—I'm not tall enough for it. Anyway,' she went on, her expression downcast once more, 'I don't like evening clothes. I'm too clumsy for them.'

'Oh, you don't seem clumsy at all!' Alexa said immediately. The girl seemed to do nothing but deprecate herself, which was completely unfair—just because she was wearing a dress that no one with any sense should have put her in.

'I am,' responded the girl. 'My mother always says so! And my fiancé thinks it—I can tell.'

Alexa frowned again. 'Surely not?'

'He does. I know,' the girl averred. 'And if he doesn't think me clumsy, he thinks me very gauche and boring, even though he tries to hide it. He's used to beautiful, elegant women. Women like you,' she said artlessly. 'But it doesn't matter.' She gave a heavy, resigned sigh. 'Because he's marrying me all the same—it's all arranged.'

Alexa felt her unease mount. Part of her knew she should not really be allowing this conversation, but part of her— the greater part—could not help but feel disquieted by this artless but clearly self-deprecating girl and what she was depicting about her engagement.

'You know, these days,' she ventured carefully, busying herself wiping her fingers on the handtowel, 'women don't *have* to marry men they've been "arranged" to marry...'

The girl only shrugged. 'Well, it's better than the alternative. Being nagged to death by my parents! They're actually pleased with me for the first time in my life— even though my mother keeps going on at me about how to behave, and so on and so on. My fiancé won't take any more notice of me when we're married than he does now— he'll keep a mistress, one of those beautiful, elegant women that he prefers. I won't mind, really.' She lifted her chin, as if to confirm her assertion, but Alexa saw a bleakness in her eyes and felt her disquiet increase.

She opened her mouth to say something, but what she didn't know—because what *could* she say? Before she could speak, someone came into the area.

'Louisa! There you are! We were about to send out a search party!'

It was a middle-aged woman with the cut-glass voice of the English upper-class. The girl Alexa had been speaking to started, as if caught out doing something she shouldn't have been.

'I'm just coming,' she said hastily, immediately looking flustered. She threw a glance at Alexa, the bleakness in her face replaced by a fleeting awkward smile, then she was gone, ushered out by the older woman, who hadn't wasted a glance at Alexa.

Slowly, Alexa dropped the used handtowel into the basket provided. She felt a pang of pity for the girl, stranger though she was. It was none of her business, obviously, but no girl who was betrothed should be that downcast. She should be brimming with happiness, radiant with joy. The last thing that poor girl looked was *radiant*...

She sighed. Life was seldom as happy as people wanted it to be. Hers included. The exchange with the girl, disturbing as it had been, had served to distract her from her own situation, but now, as she forced herself to return to the ballroom, she felt the weight of it tear at her. Misery enveloped her. Why, oh, why had she had to see Guy again? How was she to do what she knew with every fibre of her being she must do? Free herself from the hopeless mire she'd fallen into and get her life together again, put Guy de Rochemont behind her, into the past, where he had to be.

I thought I was making a start! Thought that I was finally making myself move on, leave him behind me.

But it had been fool's gold, that hope. All it had taken to rip every frail tatter of that hope had been a bare few moments...

An ache scoured inside her, physical in its impact.

Hopeless in its longing for something that could never be.

One of his party had said something to him, but Guy hadn't the faintest idea what it was. He had hardly noticed when Louisa had returned to his side. There was only one thing that he was aware of—burningly, corruscatingly aware.

He was angry.

It was inside him, lashing like the tail of a tiger. His replies to conversation grew more abstract, his mood more impatient. He needed to get out of here. He needed to get rid of these people—Louisa included. In a remote corner of his mind he knew he was being brutishly unjust, because none of this was her doing. It was not *her* fault she was standing beside him, gauche and awkward, saying so little her lack of conversational ability was almost painful. It was not *her* fault that her father had got his damn bank into deep water, and it was not *her* fault that she just happened to be Heinrich's daughter. It was not her fault that she was going to marry Guy.

Above all—and he could feel the lash of his anger catching him on the raw, castigating him—it was not her fault she was not Alexa...

Into the mesh of anger another emotion speared—an emotion he did not want to feel, as he did not want to feel this lashing within him. An emotion that he wanted to push away, deny, ignore, disregard—any word would do, so long as he got rid of it. Disposed of it. Just the way he had disposed of his affair with Alexa Harcourt with a stark, effective severing. He had moved her out of his life because she could no longer be part of it—because his life had moved on.

Into the tunnel. The tunnel that was funnelling him forward to a marriage he could not avoid, to a future mapped out for him just as it had been for his parents, Louisa's parents, and so many more of his family over the generations, across the centuries.

Anger speared again, more intense. More intense, too, the other emotion—the one that was focussed like a dark, burning flame on what he had put aside to enter the tunnel. What he could not have again.

And what, with sudden consuming heat, he wanted once more...

One last time...

CHAPTER SIX

'THANK you so much, Richard, for a lovely evening.' Alexa infused warmth into her voice. It was a little forced, but she hoped Richard hadn't noticed. Just as she hoped he hadn't noticed her abstraction during the remainder of the evening.

She'd tried hard to be a good guest, the pleasant evening companion owed to someone as nice as Richard Saxonby, but her mind had had a will of its own. It had wanted her to wander off, wanted her to seek and find the object of its attentions, and she'd had continually to rein it back. So, too, her gaze. The knowledge that Guy was somewhere in this vast gathering, with scores of tables and hundreds of people, had been a constant torment to her. She had felt herself disastrously, damningly, wanting to seek him out with her eyes, searching through the mass to see if her eyes could light on him again...feast on him again. But they mustn't! She must not. That was all there was to it.

But it might be the very last time I see him in the flesh...

The plea came from somewhere deep inside her. She fought to crush it back, push it back where it had come from, but it kept trying to find its way out.

I've got to be strong! I've got to!

The admonition was fierce, the intent resolute.

Just don't look for him—don't try and see him. Leave him alone. He's nothing to do with you any more—nothing!

That was all she must hold on to. That time in her life, when Guy de Rochemont had been with her, was over. Gone. Finished. That was all there was to it.

But it was one thing to tell herself that, another to do what she was told—stop trying to see Guy somewhere in all this crowd.

In the end it had been a relief when Richard's party had started to break up and disperse. So focussed had she been on Guy's disastrous presence at the gala that she'd given no thought to what Richard might be thinking about how the evening should end. But now, as he helped her into a taxi in the hotel's forecourt, he said solicitously, after she'd thanked him for the evening, 'Would you like me to see you home?'

It was lightly said, no more than a polite offer, and Alexa was grateful. He was not going to chance anything this early, and it was yet another sign of how nice he was. Since she knew he lived in Highgate, quite a different direction from Notting Hill, she assured him she'd be absolutely fine, thanked him again for the evening, and waved him goodbye as her taxi pulled away. But once she was on her own, the taxi threading along Park Lane, she was instantly prey to her emotions. She sat back, her eyes shut, wishing she could shut out her thoughts as easily.

But it was impossible. Impossible to suppress, as she knew she must, the swirl of emotions in her head. Oh, *why* had she had to see Guy again? It had been the very last thing she'd needed!

I thought I was starting to get over him. Get him out of my system. Move on. Make new connections, put him behind me finally...

Her eyes shadowed.

I thought I was starting to make myself fall out of love with him...

Her hopes had been real, fervent—but all it had taken was a single, shocking sight of him to know just how useless those hopes had been. In anguish, the thought resolved in her head. Hollowing her out with hopelessness.

I'm still in love with him... And there's nothing I can do about it...

The truth, stark and painful, stared bleakly back at her, scraping at her heart with razoring pain. Guy was gone—gone from her life...

As the taxi deposited her on the pavement outside the house she lived in, she felt an empty longing in her, a hopeless tearing. She opened the front door into the entrance lobby. Dolefully, her feet leaden, she gathered her narrow skirt in one hand and headed heavy-hearted up the stairs. Never had life seemed so bleak.

A pall seemed to be hanging over her, slowing her steps. And what was there to speed up for? An empty flat awaited her. A lonely night.

A hopeless skein of yearning unwound in her. Heartache and hollowness.

In her head, as it had been over and over again, she saw Guy's image and felt her heart squeeze—but Guy wasn't there. Would never be there. Never again. Never—

The ache in her heart worsened.

At the door to her flat she paused, summoning the mental energy to open it and go in. When she did, she closed the door behind her, feeling the emptiness of the flat all around her. Dropping her evening bag on the hall table, she shrugged off her fake fur evening jacket and walked listlessly into the sitting room, intent on reaching the kitchen beyond to make herself a cup of herbal tea to retire with—and stopped dead.

Guy de Rochemont was there.

Her pulse froze. Then surged. She must have made some small noise in her throat, her hand flying upwards. Did she try and speak? She didn't know. Only that Guy had cut right across her.

'Where is he?' he asked, his voice casual. But there was the edge of a whip in it.

'Who?' Alexa's brow furrowed as she tried to breathe. Tried to reel in all her senses, emotions that were suddenly flying haywire, as if an electric field had arced through the room.

Guy—Guy is here—here!

The consciousness of his presence transfixed her. Stifled her lungs.

'Lover-boy,' said Guy.

Alexa stared. Stared at the figure seated as she had seen him so often, shadowed by the dim light. She didn't answer—couldn't answer. Had no idea what he was talking about. No idea about anything at all other than the overpowering consciousness of his presence.

With a sudden fluid movement he jack-knifed to his feet, crossed towards her. His pace was feral, and Alexa felt a flare deep within her.

'You didn't bring him back here?' The voice was harsh.

The question had tormented him all the way here—all the time since he had ushered Louisa to the steps of her friend's house, bade her goodnight, his mouth saying words that were appropriate, his mind somewhere completely different.

Making his decision.

Issuing the requisite instructions to his driver.

He still had the keys to Alexa's flat, and as he'd walked in he had known that the only thing on his mind was whether she was going to come back here alone, or go home with the man who had replaced him. Or bring the man back here.

Now, with a surge of raw, visceral emotion, he knew she had done all that he'd desired—come here, and alone.

Alexa still looked blank. Was still incapable of any coherent thought at all. Only of raw, surging emotion.

A rough sound came from him, as if dismissing his own question. He closed in on her, and Alexa felt raw emotion surge again. His hands clamped on her upper arms—hard, like a vice. Her eyes flew to his. She felt that surge seize her lungs. Felt her eyes arc into his, burning green, burning into her. He was saying something to her. Something she did not understand. Whatever language it was, the words were beyond her. Everything was beyond her. She knew only the emotion surging in her, only the hard clasp of his hands on her bare flesh, only the drowning of her eyes in his.

And the feral curve of his lips as he held her, pinioned. There was an unmistakable, irrefutable message in his burning eyes. To which she could give no answer other than the one her own eyes were giving.

For one long, timeless moment he held her, as her lungs seized, frozen, unbreathing, and then slowly, achingly, agonisingly slowly, his mouth started to lower.

'No man but me, *ma belle* Alexa,' he breathed. 'No man…'

Then his mouth was branding hers with his possession.

And in his tensed, steel-coiled body, the lash of his anger was finally extinguished. The hard, unbroken armour of his iron self-control finally pierced.

* * *

It was later. Much, much later. How much later Alexa didn't know. Couldn't know. Time had stopped.

Only her senses were alive. Senses once submerged, suppressed, for four long, empty, meaningless months.

Now released again. As if from a casket, buried deep. Broken open.

Limbs splaying, spreading; hands clasping, holding; mouths seeking, devouring; bodies winding, binding. Fusing.

Fusing into one. One living, moving body. Arcing. Moulding. Melding.

On, and on, and on.

Until all was gone. All. And now she lay there, in the slackening circle of his arms, her hair a shroud around his shoulder, her brow against the smooth, damask marble of his chest, with nothing left in her. Only the plunging of her heart.

Then, into the pulsing silence, Guy spoke. His voice was rough, distanced, speaking out into the darkness around them.

'This has changed everything.' The words fell into the pounding silence between them. 'Everything,' he repeated, and his voice was harsher than ever. 'I will not do without you.' A heavy breath escaped him, his chest rising and falling. 'It will be…difficult. I cannot be with you often. Even less than I was able before. You must understand that. Accept that. It will be when I can. As I can.'

His hand around her fastened on her hip, tightened.

'It cannot be as it was. You must understand that too. But what I can do, I will.' She heard a scissoring breath. Then the voice speaking out into the darkness continued. 'I will come to you—there can be no other way. Discretion is essential—I am sorry, but it must be so. No one must know that I have taken up with you again. There can be no breath of suspicion.' She felt his chest beneath her brow rise and fall again. Then he spoke again. Still into the darkness. Staccato, disjointed. 'Then later…later…afterwards… it will be easier. It will be understood. Accepted. By everyone.' He paused again. 'Including Louisa. My intended bride.'

His voice hardened.

At his side, in his arms, Alexa felt her blood thicken and congeal.

He was still speaking. 'Until then—' He fell silent. 'Until then only this is possible,' he finished. His voice was flat.

For a while, as the blood began to sluggishly force its way through her, bringing no heat but only a chill, draining cold, she just went on lying there, her head resting on him, her hand across the flat, taut plane of his abdomen as his arms encircled her.

Imprisoned her.

He said nothing more, only gazing upwards into the darkness above them. After a while he moved, lifted one arm to glance at the circle of gold around his wrist. Then with another scissoring breath he removed himself from her, reaching for his scattered clothes, pulling them on wordlessly. She watched him—watched him with nerveless limbs, numb. When he was dressed again he looked down at her.

'I am sorry—I have to go right now. Immediately. I should not be here—not with Louisa in London. There is too much danger of discovery—too great a risk that she might find out, be informed of where I went after the gala.' He took another heavy, distracted breath. 'I will need to talk to you, *evidemment*, to explain all the arrangements, the necessities… But right now I must go. It's unavoidable. And tomorrow I'm returning to Paris. Then everything will be impossible for at least one—two weeks. Then perhaps a possibility—that is all.' His voice was still flat. 'I will phone you when I can.' His expression changed minutely. 'You can no longer phone me. You must understand that.' He broke off, then with a rasp said, 'It is the very devil, but it is the only way. The *only* way! For now there can be no other, and I will take what I can. I am sorry—but it is all that is possible now.'

For one long moment he went on looking down at her. Then with a swift, fluid movement, one hand splaying on the wall behind the bed, he sealed her mouth.

Brief, dispassionate. Marking her as his.

'Until I can get here again,' he said.

Then, straightening, he walked out.

She heard the door shut behind him. Then nothing more.

Out on the street, damp from the rain, Guy walked—his pace rapid, his mind occupied. Racing ahead. Far, far ahead. He could see it. See what he had thought he would not see again. The tunnel, opening once more to space and air. Beyond, the freedom of the eagles beckoned.

'Alexa?' Imogen's voice was sleepy. Then a moment later anxious, despite the early hour of this morning visit. It was only eight o'clock, and as it was the weekend Imogen was still in her dressing gown. She had donned it when her bell had rung, the buzzer depressed unwaveringly until Imogen had groped her way to the door and opened it. She had seen, outside, Alexa—fully dressed, a small suitcase in her hand.

And a fistful of ten-pound notes.

Alexa walked in, holding out the notes to Imogen.

'One hundred pounds,' she said. Her voice was clipped. Unemotional.

But Imogen could hear an ocean of emotion in it.

She did not take the out-held notes, only pushed Alexa into the kitchen, sat her down at the breakfast bar, plonked herself opposite. She looked at the notes, looked at Alexa, at her drawn, immobile face.

'Oh, *hell*,' said Imogen. Then, as Alexa dropped the ten ten pound notes on the bar, she added another expletive. '*Bastard*.'

A strange noise sounded in Alexa's throat.

'I didn't believe you,' she said. 'I didn't believe anything you said about him. I *wouldn't* believe it. Well, now—' she took a breath that razored the cords in her throat '—now I do.' She let her eyes rest on her friend. They were expressionless. 'You said one hundred pounds. That was the bet. One hundred pounds that he'd be back, ready to carry on, despite the minor inconvenience of his forthcoming nuptials.' She swallowed as if a stone were lodged in her throat, large and immovable. Unbearable. 'He came back. Last night. He was at the charity gala. He let himself into my flat. We—' She halted. Swallowed again. 'Then he made his proposition to me. Informed me of his plans for me. For that wretched girl he's going to marry!'

Her face worked. 'I met her last night. I didn't know it was her—and thank God she didn't know who I was! But it was clear—clear as a bell—that she knew what she was in for in marrying him. Knew just how Guy was going to treat her. I didn't know it was him she was talking about— just heard about her cold-blooded brute of a fiancé, who thinks her clumsy and gauche, and who's going to set up a mistress and pay no attention to his bride and doesn't even damn well care! Doesn't care that he's going to humiliate her and neglect her. And I felt so damn sorry for her. But I didn't…didn't…' Her features twisted. 'I didn't realise that it was going to be me who was going to be set up to be the convenient mistress. To give her husband someone "beautiful and elegant—"' she mocked the description with bitter savagery '—to have sex with, because he'd be uninterested in his *ingénue* young teenage bride!'

She raked more air into her lungs. 'Immie, I thought you were cynical and mistrusting, but you were right—right all along! I thought that however...*odd*...you thought my relationship with Guy was, you were wrong about his treating me badly. I wasn't just convenient sex-on-demand as you said I was.' Her voice hardened, scraping along her skin. 'But you were right all along. That's exactly what I was. Exactly what he still wants me to be. The only difference is that this time—' she gave a harsh, humourless laugh '—I'm to be even more invisible! This time around I mustn't even phone him, mustn't contact him, must be totally unseen, unsuspected.' Her voice twisted. 'At least until he's got this convenient extra-marital sexual arrangement accepted by his bride. Which she will, poor kid, because it's what she's expecting anyway.'

Her face worked again, hands clenching.

'Oh, Immie—how could I have been such a damn *fool*?'

Across the breakfast bar, Imogen could only sigh heavily, squeeze Alexa's hands comfortingly, and say, with care and tact, 'It's always easy to blind ourselves to what we don't want to know.' Then, with even more care and tact, she said, 'Um, you mentioned that Guy let himself in? Which means he must still have your keys? I don't mean to panic you, but it might be a good idea to change the lock.'

Alexa gazed across at her friend. Her expression changed.

'Oh,' she said, 'I'm going to do a lot more than just that.'

* * *

Guy was in a good mood. An excellent mood. The best mood he'd been in for a long time.

Everyone noticed it. His staff, his friends, his family. He knew what they ascribed his good mood to, and he found it *fort amusant* that they did. Because it had nothing to do with his impending nuptials.

Just the opposite.

Marriage to Louisa no longer loured over his head like a heavy weight. Now, thankfully, he no longer had only its confines ahead of him. Instead, he had something very different. Satisfaction creamed through him. Why had he ever thought he'd have to relinquish his liaison with Alexa? Do without her? She'd suited him so well. Why had he ever terminated his affair with her just because he had been hog-tied by Heinrich into marrying his daughter to save his pernicious bank? Such a sacrifice was, in fact, quite unnecessary.

Oh, it would be tricky, he knew. Not easy to pull off, and requiring careful timing and finesse. Yes, it would involve deceiving Louisa—but, young as she was, she had been born to a family in which such arrangements were unexceptional, so why should she object to what he was planning? She understood the realities of the kinds of lives they all led, the privileges and the obligations alike. And, since she was no more in love with him than he with her, why should she care either way? Yes, she might perceive his arrangement as unflattering, but there was no question that she would be jealous, or feel rejected. Why should she not be accommodating about it all? Understand what he was doing, and why?

As for Alexa, she had already proved exemplarily discreet, so he had no reason to doubt *her* continuance on that score. He'd warned her that extra discretion would be required initially, but he was confident it would not be an issue for her. She would be as accommodating as Louisa, understanding the necessity for a low profile for the time being.

His mind raced ahead.

When can I be with her again?

Anticipation licked in him. The hunger of desire—desire that had burned within him that night of the charity gala when he'd seen her again after doing without her for four long months. He'd told himself that terminating their affair had been a necessity he could not avoid—unwelcome though it had been when she was so exactly what suited him—but seeing her again like that he had known, when the revealing anger lashed within him, that one thing was very clear about Alexa.

No man but me.

Well, now it was going to stay that way. No man but he in her life.

That was what he wanted—and that was now what he was going to get.

He just had to make it work, that was all. And he would. Of that he was confident.

He leant back in his chair, reaching out to the keyboard on his desk, tapping it briefly to pull up his diary, scrolling rapidly down the coming weeks. He looked for that all-essential window when he could get back to London—back to Alexa.

Back to her bed.

He paused the scroll. There—that was the opportunity he wanted. Ten days away. A mere ten days to wait before he got her to himself again. His good mood enhanced, he extracted his mobile and dialled hers. There was no answer. He gave a slight shrug, sliding the phone back in his jacket pocket. He would try again later. Because of this new, irritating need for discretion he would not leave a message, only speak to her—though he knew from previous experience that when she was painting, whether or not her subject was a commission or personal, she would not answer.

Tant pis—there was time in hand.

But as the days slipped by he was still not able to reach her. Three days before he was due in London his mounting irritation peaked, and he sent one of his security staff to convey the information about his imminent arrival.

The information was never delivered.

Alexa Harcourt, so he was informed by his security staff, no longer lived at that address. Alexa Harcourt, so his disbelieving enquiries further revealed, had disappeared off the face of the earth.

CHAPTER SEVEN

ALEXA flexed her fingers, trying to warm them and failing. The cold was biting, eating into her, making holding a paintbrush an increasing ordeal. The lone electric heater in the room she'd allocated as a studio, actually little more than a lean-to, made scant impact against the harsh weather outside.

But this desolate spot was exactly what she'd sought—somewhere to hide from the man who wanted to keep her as a handy side-dish for his tasteless marriage to a girl who was resigned to his infidelity even before her wedding day. Somewhere to hide from the man who'd treated her as a convenient source of sex-on-demand, accepting and acquiescent, whenever it had suited him.

A man who expected her to say yes to anything he wanted of her.

Her face hardened. Well, finally, *finally,* she'd learnt to say no.

The tight band around her heart, which had been there for so long now, tightened another notch. She'd learnt to welcome it, that crushing tightness. Knowing that it was like a stay around her heart, holding it together. Holding her together. Making her strong.

Strong enough to hate the man she'd once loved.

Because hate him she did. There was no doubt about that. No doubt in her mind whatsoever.

He treated you like dirt—and then he came back to treat you even worse than dirt!

All the arguments that she'd poured out at Imogen's that long, nightmare day when she'd fled to her friend's house, churning with emotion, sounded again in her head. Imogen had let her pour them out, let her purge herself, and then, making her a large, hot, strong mug of tea, she'd run through all the options that presented themselves.

This cottage in the middle of winter, in the middle of nowhere, had not been top of Imogen's list. Top of her list, Alexa knew, was simply changing the locks on Alexa's flat, changing her mobile and landline number, paying a solicitor to write to Guy de Rochemont informing him not to attempt any further contact with his client, and then, as a perfect remedy to all of Alexa's ills, going out with Richard Saxonby as often as it took for her to realise he was a perfect match, then moving in with him, settling down and, best of all, marrying him.

'He's absolutely ideal for you!' Imogen had waxed lyrical, running through, yet again, all the reasons why he was such a wonderful man and perfect for Alexa.

But Alexa knew that his main attraction, for her friend, was that he was not Guy. That was all that really mattered to Imogen. Keeping Guy away from Alexa, keeping him out of her life. Out of her head. Most importantly of all, out of her heart.

'Thank goodness he's shown his true colours—not that I was ever in doubt anyway,' she seethed. 'But now even you, blind as you were to him, have seen him for what he is!'

To Imogen it was obvious, Alexa could see, that the way

to rid herself of Guy de Rochemont was by replacing him with Richard. But for Alexa it was not that simple.

'It wouldn't be fair on Richard,' she said. 'And anyway...' her chest heaved '...I don't want to be in London. It's too—'

Dangerous—that was what she meant to say. Too dangerous. Oh, she could change her locks and her telephone numbers, but that wouldn't make her feel safe.

Safe from Guy—safe from what he wanted of her.

Memory burned like a flame, licking over her flesh. It was agony—and worse, far worse, than agony....

She shut her eyes, trying to stamp out the flame, stamp out the memory imprinted onto her body. *Her body fusing with his, melding, becoming one, becoming whole...*

Desperately she tore her mind away, forcing her eyes to open again. Imogen was talking, immediately sympathetic. 'I agree—a change of scene is exactly what you need. Somewhere completely different. A holiday—you haven't had one in ages. Somewhere tropical—the Caribbean, the Maldives, the Seychelles!' Seeing her friend's expression, she hurried on. 'We'll go together. I can rearrange my diary today—there's nothing I can't get out of—then we'll hit the internet and book online. We can be at the airport tomorrow!'

'I don't think—' Alexa started hesitantly. What Imogen was suggesting was the very last thing she would possibly want.

'It's just what you need,' Imogen repeated. 'A complete change of scene, total relaxation. Getting away from everything—especially that adulterous bastard!'

Alexa shook her head. 'I want to move out of London,' she said.

Imogen was aghast. 'You can't run away! Why *should*

you? *He's* the one that's been a despicable rat. Why should you have to go? What about your commissions?'

'I've nearly finished the current one, and you'll just have to cancel anything else.'

Imogen bit her lip. 'I won't let you mess up your career for that creep.'

Alexa just looked at her. 'I've no heart for it any more. I don't want anything more to do with that world. All those rich, powerful men… It…it reminds me too much…'

'OK,' Imogen allowed, hearing the shaky note in Alexa's voice. 'Well, why not go on some kind of art-break, or something, for the rest of the winter? Move to Morocco, or Brazil, somewhere you can just paint your own stuff for a couple of months? I'll postpone any bookings and say you've gone somewhere warm for your health for the time being.'

Alexa nodded slowly, murmuring agreement, and Imogen was reassured. But she was aghast when she discovered just what Alexa had decided on.

'No, no, no, *no*!' she cried. 'That's just *not* what you need. Holing up in some godforsaken hovel in the wilds of Devon in the middle of winter!'

But her objections fell on deaf ears. Alexa packed her suitcase, and enough of her art materials to keep her going, put away the personal effects in her apartment, and handed it over to an estate agent to let it for six months. Then she hired a car, loaded it up, and set off.

'The estate agent has my contact details, but I've told him not to let you have them unless it's a genuine life or death emergency,' she told an appalled Imogen.

'I can't believe you're doing this,' Imogen said disbelievingly.

'I need to do it.' It was all Alexa could manage to say.

It had been true, and was true still, she knew, despite the

drear, cheerless countryside—or because of it. The leafless trees, the cold, raw weather, the grey, lowering skies and bare, muddy fields tuned in exactly with what she felt.

Desolate.

A desolation of the heart. Of the spirit.

Worse, much worse than before.

Then I thought it was simply that I'd fallen in love with a man who hadn't fallen in love with me. I accepted it—just as I accepted the limitations of the relationship—but I never thought ill of him.

The vice around her heart crushed tighter still.

Now she knew better.

She knew that she'd fallen in love with a man who wanted nothing more than adulterous, clandestine sexual congress. He regarded her as fit for nothing more. Humiliating his bride, holding both her and the woman he wanted to make sexual use of in callous contempt.

For a man like that it was possible to feel only one emotion.

Not love. Never love—not for a man like that. Love had to be not ignored, like last time, not starved or blanked out, but torn out by its roots, ripped out of her heart, bleed though it would. It did not matter. She had to be clean of such a tainted, toxic emotion. For such a man only one emotion should be felt.

Hatred. Hatred that would burn her clean—burn and rip that misbegotten love out of her. Hatred that could tear it loose.

Hatred that could free her from its thrall. Release her from this prison of desolation.

But hatred had to be channelled, or it would devour her.

With a set, granite face she reached again for the canvas. Blank, bare—

Then reached for her paints, her brush.

Reached for her hatred.

And let it loose upon the canvas.

'Well?' Guy's voice was harsh as he snatched up the phone.

'It's done.' The person at the other end of the line was brief, the way he knew his employer wanted him to be. He'd given the answer he knew his employer wanted. Just why Guy de Rochemont, who ran the vast financial and commercial empire of Rochemont-Lorenz, wanted to make this particular purchase his employee had no idea. It fitted in with nothing in the vast Rochemont-Lorenz portfolio, and was on such a small scale that even if there had been some logical reason for it, it was hardly of the order of magnitude that would draw the attention of the head of the empire. But it was not his job to ask questions—only to carry out instructions, and that was what he had done.

'Now, get me the following information,' came his next instruction down the line. 'I want it by tonight.' The line went dead.

In his London office, Guy dropped the phone on the gleaming mahoghany surface of his desk. His eyes stared out into the middle distance. They were very green. Very glittering.

Hard as emeralds.

They were harder still when he received the information he'd demanded. Still hard when the next morning, after a sleepless night—as so many nights now were—he climbed into the gleaming new vehicle and gunned the engine, keying in his destination to the satnav.

As he headed out into the London traffic the emerald glitter focussed only on the direction he was going.

Westwards.

* * *

It had been raining all night. Steady, relentless rain that had come down out of a leaden sky, turning the fields to a quagmire and the unmetalled lane up to the cottage to little better. Alexa was glad she didn't have to get in any shopping for a while. She'd got into a routine since she'd been here, of driving into the local market town some ten miles away and picking up enough groceries and household items to keep her going for a week.

Her lifestyle was simple, pared to the bone. She was uninterested in anything else. So long as the stash of logs neatly stacked in the outhouse extension behind the cottage's old-fashioned kitchen held out, so she could feed the log-burning stove in the sitting room that was the main source of heat besides the electric heater in the lean to, and so long as the electricity supply stayed operational, she was fine.

She wasn't lonely.

She was used, after all, to a quiet lifestyle. Even in London she'd been content with her own company, never craving the bright lights. Occasional dinner parties, lunch out, the theatre, concerts and art exhibitions were all that she'd wanted. Had it not been for her work and for the rich treasures of art that London housed she'd have been happier in the country anyway.

Though she would not want to live anywhere as remote, as desolate as this isolated cottage. It was doubtless an idyllically pastoral hideway in the summer for holiday-makers, but it now dripped water from the eaves on her head when she stepped outside. From under the doors a perpetual draught whistled, echoing the wind wuthering in the chimney in the evenings. The windows rattled in the bedroom, and she was pretty certain that mice were scuttling in the cob walls.

Not that they bothered her either, provided they kept out

of sight. Nor did the spiders that emerged from the wood basket, scuttling across the sitting room to take refuge under the sofa.

Unless the rain was a deluge, she made the effort to get outdoors every day, pulling on the pair of sturdy gumboots she'd bought in the market town, with a thick waxed jacket and a scarf to hold her hair down in the wind that blew in from the west, whatever the weather. She tramped down the muddy lanes and across fields, where incurious cattle continued to graze, and weather-beaten sheep lifted heads to stare unblinkingly at her as she crossed their domain.

The bleakness all around her echoed her own.

How long had she been here now? The days had merged one into another, and then into weeks. It must be four, five weeks already.

But time had no meaning for her. She was living in a world of her own, bare and bleak, but it was what she wanted. What she needed.

She crossed to the log-burner and crouched down to feed it. She'd mastered the art of keeping it alight, damping down all night, then building it up again in the morning. Now, by midday, the little sitting room was warm, despite the raw cold outside and the sodden, chill air.

Closing the door of the log-burner, she straightened. And turned her head sharply. She could hear a car approaching.

It was a car, definitely, not the tractor in which the local farmer sometimes lumbered past the cottage on his way to his fields. Warily, she crossed to the little deep inset window and peered out across the lane. A huge four-by-four was drawing up, its sides covered in newly spattered mud from the unmetalled lane, its wheels half a foot deep in a waterlogged rut.

Was this the letting agent? The local farmer? Someone

who was completely lost down this dead-end lane? Someone was getting out. She heard a car door slam, but she couldn't see from this side. She quit her post and headed for the front door, pulling it open.

And froze.

Disbelief drowned her. She could *not* be seeing what she was. She couldn't...

It can't be him—it can't, it can't! It's impossible. Impossible! He can't be here. He can't, he can't, he can't!

But he was. Striding up to her.

Her vision swam, and she clutched at the doorframe to steady herself. He stopped in front of her, Tall. Over-powering.

Intimidating.

A shot of emotion bolted through her. It wasn't fear—it couldn't be fear, surely it couldn't be fear? But it was strong, and sharp and it seized her lungs.

'Alexa.'

It was all he said, standing there, confronting her.

'How—how did you...?' Her frail voice failed.

But he didn't answer, merely steered past her, going into the cottage. Numbly she followed him. He seemed far too tall for its low-pitched confines. He strode into the living room, where the log-burner beckoned, and positioned himself in front of it, looking around the room. Then his gaze swept back to Alexa, standing frozen by the doorway. His eyes glittered.

'Why?'

A single word, but to Alexa it held a universe of demand. Shock was still seizing her, but she'd gone into that ultra-calm that accompanied the condition. Everything seemed to have stopped around her.

'Why?' she echoed. Her voice seemed calm too. Preternaturally calm. 'Why what, precisely, Guy?'

'Why did you run?' His voice was less controlled than hers. Deeper. Harsher. And his eyes still burned green.

Alexa tilted her head. Very slightly, but discernibly. 'What did I have to stay for? Your…offer…didn't appeal.'

His eyes narrowed, pinpointing her with laser focus. 'No? That wasn't the message I got when I had your body beneath mine. You gave me a quite different message then, Alexa.' His voice caressed her like the tip of a whip.

She felt colour flare in her cheeks. 'That shouldn't have happened.'

'But it did. It did, Alexa, and now I want an explanation of what the *hell* you think you're doing!'

He was angry. He was actually angry. Alexa stared at him. Inside, she felt a leashed, powerful emotion at seeing him standing here, in the very place she had sought refuge from him. But she would not let it loose. She would keep it smothered. Controlled.

'How did you find me?' Her voice was clipped. 'No one knows I'm here.'

'Your letting agency knows. I found them through the tenants in your flat.' His tone was offhand.

'I instructed the agency to disclose this address to no one!' she snapped. 'How dared they tell you?'

His eyes glinted sardonically. 'I have access to all their files. As of yesterday, the agency belongs to me.'

'*What?*'

'I bought the agency, Alexa. It was clearly the only way to find out where you were.'

She stared. 'You *bought* the agency to get my address?' There was incredulity in her voice. Then, with a lift of her chin, she bit out, 'You wasted your money. I don't know what you think you're doing, but—'

'I'm doing what I clearly ought to have done that night—making things clear to you!'

Her eyes flashed. 'Oh, you made things very clear—don't worry. I got the picture, I promise you. But like I said, I didn't like the offer, so I turned it down. And now—' her face hardened '—you can just get out—get out of my life!'

His expression changed. 'You don't mean that.'

It was the calm assurance with which he spoke that lit the touchpaper. Exploding her fury.

'My God,' she breathed, 'you arrogant, conceited pig! Do you really think that just because you're Guy de Rochemont you can behave any way you want? Do you think that just because like a complete *idiot* I fell back into bed with you I'll do whatever you want? Do you? You think you can have an affair with me, and then calmly tell me one fine day that you're getting married, and that's it—and then months later turn up again and just pick up again where you left off, not worrying about anything as trivial as your fiancée? *Do* you? Because—'

'Stop—Alexa, listen to me.' His hand had flown up, as if to silence her passionate outpouring with an autocratic command.

'What for?' she bit back. 'So you can tell me how *discreet* you're going to have to be when you pick up with me again?'

His eyes flashed. 'I can't help that, Alexa! Do you think I *want* to be clandestine in that way? I have no choice. And if you will simply *listen* to me, I will explain why—'

'Oh, I'm sure you will!' she thrust witheringly. 'To you it's all totally straightforward, isn't it? Well, it is to me too. I don't want anything more to do with you. There is nothing, *nothing* you can say that will change that. So go—*go!*'

She could feel her heart pounding in her chest, adrenaline pumping. It was unbearable—unbearable that Guy had walked in here.

'Just *go!*' she repeated, because he hadn't budged at all, was still standing there, looking like the lord of the manor in the humble cottage of one of his countless peasants. Rich, arrogant, conceited—thinking he only had to find her to dictate his terms to her again.

'Just *go!* You pushed your way in here. It's unbelievable! You actually went and bought the letting agency just to find me. Your ego is monstrous—monstrous! Just because you're Guy de Rochemont, born with a whole canteen of silver spoons in your mouth, and just because women swoon at your feet, you think you can do anything you want, get anyone you want. Any woman you want. Well, not me—not any more! There is nothing, *nothing* you can say to me that would *ever* change my mind.'

His face was stark as she threw her bitter words at him. Two white lines flared along his cheekbones.

'Then I won't waste my time talking.'

He was in front of her in an instant. He seized her arms, lowering over her. Panic, rage, fury, convulsed her. She threw herself backwards.

'*No!* Not this time. Don't touch me.' She took a shuddering, shaking breath. 'Whatever we had, it's over. I'm not going there again. Ever. I don't *care,*' she spelt out, her words cutting like stone knives, hard and heavy, 'whether you have a tame, cowed little fiancée in tow or not. I don't want anything to do with you.' Her face worked. 'You were bad news right from the start, though I was too stupid to see it—and you're bad news now. You always will be. I don't want you. I don't want anything to do with you. On any terms.' She took one last shuddering breath. 'Any terms at all.'

Her voice was flat. Final. She stared at him. She was back under control now. Back from that dangerous maelstrom of emotion. She'd mastered it, quelled it.

His face was stark, his jaw set like steel, the white lines along his tensed cheekbones etched like acid. His eyes were unreadable. Completely unreadable.

They always were. I never knew him. I loved him, but I never knew him. How stupid can a woman be, to love a man she doesn't know? Who keeps her out of his real life...

Pain twisted inside her. All she'd ever had of him had been brief, bare snatches. Making do with scraps. No wonder he'd thought she would accept that vile adulterous offer of his. He'd had every expectation she would comply. After all, all he had to do was seduce her, just as he'd done that first time, and she would acquiesce in anything he wanted.

But no more. No *more.*

The desolation she was long familiar with swept through her. This had to end—now. His eyes were on her. Masked. Unreadable. The pain twisted again—the pain of seeing him, wanting so much to reach out and let him take her in his arms, let his mouth lower to hers, let him do what every cell in her body suddenly, flaringly, vividly, oh, so vividly, wanted him to do—let him make her forget everything that her head knew about him, everything that she must not forget. To melt her flesh and melt her mind, so that they were only bodies, bared and beautiful, twining together, made one together...

But they weren't one. They were as separate from each other as it was possible to be.

'Alexa—'

There was something in his voice. Something that she blocked out. Had to block out. Something dangerous.

'No.' She shook her head. 'No—I'm not going there. This ends, Guy. Now.'

She moved away, making the move deliberate, controlled. Heading for the kitchen and the lean-to beyond.

'At least your journey won't be wasted. I've no idea whether you still want this, but I know I don't.' Her voice was cold—as cold as she could make it.

Her painting equipment was in the lean-to, and resting on a chair was the object she was going to fetch. He might as well take it now—it would save her having to courier it at some point, whenever the time came when she could no longer hole up here in the middle of nowhere. She'd wrapped it up already. She didn't want to look at it. She'd finished it—the ability to do so had come to her, and she knew why it had, and hated herself—and it—for that very reason. But then, and only then, had it released her from its loathsome power....

She gathered the parcel up and turned, ready to take it out to him. But he had followed her. He wasn't looking at her, however. Not even at the object she was holding. He was looking to the canvas on her easel.

She stilled.

His face was immobile. Silently she held out the wrapped painting in her hands to him. It was his portrait. The one she'd not been able to do. Now she had.

But not on its own. The portrait—quite deliberately and intentionally—was one of a pair.

Its companion was still on the easel. As finished as it would ever be.

His eyes were fixed on it, and in them Alexa saw a shadow flicker deep, deep within. Something moved in her, something even deeper inside her than the shadow in his eyes. Something even darker.

'That one I'm keeping,' she said. Her voice had no emotion in it. The emotion was all in the paint on the canvas.

In the twisted, demonic image of his face. The face of a man she had once loved.

But now only hated.

'It's to remind me of you,' she said.

For a second, an instant, his eyes went to her. But there was nothing in them. Nothing she could discern. The mask over them was complete.

He took the wrapped portrait—the other one, the one that bore the face that Guy de Rochemont showed to the world. To the women in his bed.

Then, slowly, he inclined his head to her. 'I won't trouble you again, Alexa.'

There was nothing in his voice just as there was nothing in his eyes.

He turned and left. Walking out. Out of her life.

Leaving only the dark portrait to keep her company.

Slowly, haltingly, she went back into the sitting room. The fire was still blazing fiercely in the log-burner, and she could feel the warmth after the chill of the lean to.

But she was shivering all the same.

Guy drove. The long motorway back to London stretched before him, and the powerful car ate up the miles. On either side of the motorway the drear wintry landscape stretched, monotonous and rainswept. Grey and bleak.

Just like his life.

It stretched out ahead of him—swallowing him up.

He had seen hope—hope almost within reach, within his grasp and he'd stretched out his hands to take it.

Seize it.

Instead—

Instead it had been like a shot through the skull. Instant, total destruction. The work of a second. All it had taken for his eyes to light on, to focus on that square of canvas resting on the easel.

A mirror—a mirror held up to him.

In the few brief moments when his eyes had rested on it he had known—searingly, punishingly—that Alexa was gone. Out of his life.

She would never come back into it.

He pressed the accelerator, increasing the speed taking him away from her. Back to all that was left to him now.

His hands tightened on the steering wheel. Alexa was lost to him—he could not have her on any terms. She had shown him that in a square of canvas.

So now a heaviness settled over him, a weariness. All he could do was continue on the course he had resolved on. Ahead of him waited the girl he had said he would marry. He would do what he could for her.

What else was there for him to do? With Alexa gone—nothing.

Only Louisa.

CHAPTER EIGHT

SPRING came. The days lengthened, the tender shoots of new growth peered between the blasted stalks of last year's vegetation. In the garden and in the hedgerows primroses pushed their way out of the dark, confining earth, new leaves unfurled on bared branches. Life returned.

And Alexa returned to London.

But not to live. Only to pause, then pack again, and head to Heathrow. She'd booked a desert safari—a tough one. Bumping across endless dunes in a Jeep, sleeping in a bedroll underneath the stars which burned through the floor of heaven, revealing blisters of brightness, cracks showing the existence of a realm impossible to reach.

By day the sun burned down, hazing the horizon so that it was impossible to know if the Jeep were making progress or not. Yet each day they were a little further on. Each day a little further from their starting point.

They reached their goal—old ruins of an ancient city that had once been filled with living, breathing people, each one of them with their own life, their own aspirations, hopes and dreams, their own dreads and losses. Now only the desert dust blew through their emptied houses, along their deserted streets.

Alexa stopped and stared out over the desolation. Lines, bleak and spare, tolled in her head.

"'For the world...hath really neither joy, nor love...nor peace, nor help for pain...'"

No, there was no help for pain, she knew. But the cruellest lines of the poem she could not say: *'Ah, love, let us be true to one another...'*

Could not even think them. Could only envy the poet who'd had someone to be true to, someone true to him.

Beyond the city's ruins, the bare and boundless desert sands stretched far away, and she stood looking out over their loneliness, encircled in isolation, filled with a quiet despair.

And a new resolution. This could not go on—this endless desolation. It could not. Or it would destroy her. Somehow she had to find the strength to get past it. She had done it once before, when her parents had been killed, and she had found the strength to renew her life. Whatever it took, she had to do it again now.

So, at the end of the safari, when the Jeep returned to base, she did not head for the airport with the others. She found a small *pension*, simple but respectable, and stayed there awhile, going out every day with paints and inks and sketchbook, her body shrouded to keep attention from her, her head covered against both the sun and male eyes. The locals thought her mad but let her be, unmolested and unchallenged, and she was grateful.

Each day she worked, depicting in starkest lines the empty vastness of the lifeless desert, and each day, in the dry, relentless heat, little by little the endless pain in her desiccated a little more, a little more.

Until she could feel it no longer.

Had it gone completely? She couldn't tell. Only knew, with a deep, sure certainty, that the work she had done was good. Spare, stark, bare. But good.

Then and only then did she pack up her work and head

for home. The six-month lease of her tenants had expired, and they had moved out. She was wary, deeply so, of returning to London, lest it plunge her back into the vortex of memory again. Above all she knew that she would not—could not—simply return to the life she had had. She would put the flat on the market, move away, right out of London, for good. Find a future in her work.

It was hard to walk into her flat. Hard to see its familiar contours. Hard to block out the memories that went with it. But block them she did. Not bothering to unpack, she left her suitcase in the bedroom, with her newly created portfolio of desert art, and took a quick shower to refresh herself after her long flight. Then she changed into a pair of well-cut grey trousers and an ice-blue jersey top, knotted her hair into its usual neat chignon, took up her handbag and went back downstairs.

She needed to go to the shops to refill the fridge. On the way back she would look in at the estate agents—*not* the agency that Guy had so arrogantly bought!—and talk about marketing her flat for immediate sale. In the evening she would go through all her finances to see what her options for the future would be. At some point, too, she knew she would have tell Imogen she was back—but not until she had a good idea of what her plans were going to be. Her mind busy, determinedly so, she stepped out of the front door and headed down the short flight of steps to the pavement.

'Miss Harcourt—'

A car had pulled up in front of her at the kerb, and a man was getting out. The car was nondescript, and so was the man accosting her. In broad daylight, on a busy pavement, her only emotion was puzzlement.

'Yes?' she said.

'I work for a security firm,' the man said. He handed her a business card, with an upmarket-looking name on it that even she had vaguely heard of. 'My client has requested a meeting with you.'

'What client?' said Alexa. Warning bells were ringing now.

'Madame de Rochemont,' said the man.

Alexa froze. Madame de Rochemont. Guy's wife.

Despite the heat of the afternoon, a chill went through her. A chill she forced to subside. She had not spent all that time away, purging herself of the past, only to be felled at the first reminder of what was no longer a part of her life, a part of her. But her insides churned for all her resolution.

He had a wife.

It was done—Guy was married.

Married to that poor girl—the one who'd looked the antithesis of 'radiant' at the prospect. With good reason. Alexa's mouth thinned. Louisa von Lorenz had known what kind of man she was marrying. What kind of marriage she was in for. What kind of husband she was getting.

The adulterous kind.

Alexa's thoughts were like knives. But why on earth should Guy's wretched new wife have asked for a meeting with *her*? What for?

How does she even know of my existence?

And how could she possibly know I'd be walking along this pavement today?

'How,' demanded Alexa frigidly, 'does Madame de Rochemont come to know of my whereabouts?'

The man was unfazed by the question. Maybe it was a familiar one to someone in his line of work. 'When your tenants moved out, Miss Harcourt, your flat was put under surveillance on the chance you might be returning shortly. As indeed you have.'

Alexa's mouth twisted. Of course. Guy had bought the lettings agency, hadn't he? When you moved in the stratospheric circles that the de Rochemont family moved in such things were unexceptional. Just like hiring people like this man to wait until she showed up.

But how Guy's wife had found her was inconsequential—the question was why on earth did Louisa de Rochemont want to meet her?

Cold went through her suddenly as realisation struck.

Does she think I'm going to take up with Guy again now that I'm back in London? Is that what she fears?

Had that poor girl somehow found out—or been told—just who the last woman was that her husband had had a liaison with before he'd become engaged? Had she then, knowing what her husband was going to be like, speculated that he might well carry on after their engagement and their marriage with the same woman he'd been seeing before?

The chill in Alexa's veins deepened. Had all this security surveillance and private investigation shown up a photo of her? It was more than likely. And then—she swallowed horribly—then Louisa would recognise her from that evening at the charity gala.

She'll know that she spoke to me—will she think that I knew all along who she was?

But, whether Louisa had seen Alexa's photo or not, Alexa knew that one thing was clear—she was not going to have Guy's bride think the worst of her. Whoever was providing Guy's adulterous sex, it was not her! And any attempts, by any of them, to subject her to surveillance and investigation could stop right now! She was clear of Guy de Rochemont and she would stay that way. She would not be sucked back anywhere near that maelstrom. Wasn't she doing everything she could to be free of it all?

She looked straight at the man. 'Where is your client?' she demanded.

'Madame de Rochemont is currently in London, Miss

Harcourt,' he answered, in his professionally neutral tone. 'She has indicated that it would suit her to see you this afternoon.'

London? Well, that was convenient. And so was getting this over and done with right now. Another thing she could put behind her.

'Very well.' She pulled open the rear door of the car and climbed in. The man got into the driving seat and restarted the engine. The car set off, heading out onto Ladbroke Grove, and thence towards Holland Park. Cutting across Kensington, it made its way into the pristine, elegant squares of Belgravia, pulling up outside a vast white-stuccoed terraced house set on an elegant square with a private garden in the centre. It was a location where, Alexa knew, only the richest of the rich could afford to live. But then, Guy de Rochemont *was* in that ultra-exclusive echelon.

I knew he was rich, but I hardly saw it, Alexa thought as she got out of the car. So was it really so surprising that a man like that, so blessed by the gods—not just with vast wealth and the highest social position, but by incredible good-looks and searing masculine attraction—should have thought that she, or any woman, his wife included, would do whatever he wanted of them, without question or demur or objection? Would such a man not naturally have a natural arrogance that expected others to comply with his every wish, every desire?

Like the way she'd just rolled over into his bed the moment he'd indicated he wanted her there...

But even as she thought that memory intervened. Not the memory of Guy casually informing her that he'd bought a lettings agency as he might buy a bar of chocolate, simply in order to locate her, or informing her that she had been selected to provide his sexual amusement and compensate for his being required to marry a teenager for dynastic purposes, or demanding to know what the hell she thought she was playing at by objecting to his plans for her.

Not that Guy.

The Guy who took me to bed—breathtakingly, wonderfully, amazingly! The Guy who held me afterwards, slept with me, woke with me. Ate with me, smiled at me, talked with me about art and history and culture. Who would sit and check his e-mails on his laptop, or look through business papers, while I watched a TV documentary or read a book. Nothing much, nothing extraordinary.

Yet precious—so precious…

The old, familiar rending ache scraped at her. She had to wrest it away, make herself think of Guy as she had to think of him now.

Above all, a married man.

A married man whose wife—young, naïve, innocent—did not deserve to have her marriage, as difficult as it must be, blighted even more by worrying about whether her husband was going to take up with his former lover again. A wife who, though she might call a house in Belgravia only one of what were doubtless half a dozen palatial homes around the world, deserved the reassurance that only Alexa could give her.

Yet as Alexa walked up the wide steps of the multi-million pound house, stepping into the grand hallway beyond, she felt anew the gaping distance between the world she moved in and the world that Guy and his bride inhabited. She had been kept far apart from it.

He's a world away from me—he always was.

Like a spear in her side, she felt the force of how pointless it had been to fall in love with such a man.

Reluctance at being here filled her. But this had to be done. Head held high, she followed the member of staff who had admitted her as he proceeded up a graceful sweep of stairs to the first floor. She was ushered into a vast drawing room.

She stopped short, her eyes going instantly to the walls. It was the paintings that drew her first, not the opulence of the Louis Quinze decor. She heard her breath catch as she took in enough priceless artworks to fill a small museum. Fragonard, Watteau, Boucher, Claude, Poussin—

Instinctively, without realising she was doing so, she walked up to the one closest to her and gazed at it. A riot of Rococo art, a *fête galante*, with girls in clouds of silks and satins, and young men as lavishly adorned. A fantasy of the Ancien Régime that took her breath away with the exquisite delicacy of its brushstrokes to catch the richness of the fabrics, the hues of the fruits and flowers.

A voice spoke behind her.

'Rococo is no longer fashionable, but I confess I have a particular fondness for it. It embodies all that is most *charmant* in art.'

The voice that spoke had the crystal quality of the upper classes, but with a distinct French accent. It was not the voice of the young girl that Alexa had encountered in the powder room at the charity gala. She swivelled round.

A woman who must have been in late middle age, but who had the figure of a woman no more than thirty, chicly dressed, was standing before a huge marble fireplace, on an Aubusson rug, between two silk-upholstered facing sofas. Her dress was a couture design, Alexa could see instantly, and several ropes of pearls were wound around her neck. Her hair was tinted, immaculately styled, and her *maquillage* was perfect.

And her eyes were green. As green as emeralds.

Alexa started.

'Yes,' said the woman, acknowledging why Alexa had reacted. 'My son has inherited his eye colour from me.'

Her son—?

Alexa swallowed. *Madame de Rochemont…*

She had assumed—of course she had assumed—that it could only be Guy's wife.

The woman who was not Guy's wife—who was his mother, could *only* be his mother—walked forward several steps, holding out her hand. Alexa found herself walking forward as well, to take it briefly.

'Won't you sit down, Mademoiselle Harcourt?'

With a posture that was regally elegant, Madame de Rochemont indicated one of the pair of silk covered sofas. As Alexa lowered herself down, her head in a whirl, Guy's mother took her place opposite her. Her green eyes flicked briefly over Alexa's habitually groomed appearance, as if she were assessing her.

Alexa's thoughts were reeling. What on earth was going on? Why was she here? Why on earth had Guy's *mother* wanted to see her?

'Thank you so much for coming, Mademoiselle Harcourt. I have wanted to meet you for some time.'

Alexa could only stare, nonplussed. All her expectations had been overset, and she could make no sense of what was happening. Then, a moment later, enlightenment dawned.

'I wanted to thank you in person,' Madame de Rochemont said, 'for the portrait you made of Guy. He presented it to me for my birthday last month. I am very pleased with it.'

'I…I'm so glad,' Alexa managed to get out.

'And I am also,' said Guy's mother, and now there was a different note in her voice which Alexa could not place, 'very grateful for it.'

Alexa gazed at her. For a long moment, Madame de Rochemont simply looked back at her. Alexa had the strangest feeling she was being placed in a balance and weighed. Then, abruptly, the moment ended.

'I understand you have been traveling?' said Madame de Rochemont. 'The Middle East. An unusual choice for a young woman.'

'I—I wanted somewhere different,' Alexa managed to say, wondering why Guy's mother should have gone to the trouble of finding out where she had been these last weeks.

'Indeed. But it is not a part of the world where young women tend to go on their own,' observed Madame de Rochemont.

Still reeling, Alexa tried to gather enough composure to make an appropriate answer. 'I was treated with great respect, *madame*—I did not court attention in any way, and my hosts were kindness itself.'

'You were there some time?'

'I worked, *madame*. Painted. The desert has a beauty of its own.'

'Of course. Tell me, do you plan to exhibit your work?'

Alexa shook her head. 'My talent, such as it is, is moderate only. Portraiture allowed me a comfortable standard of living, and I am grateful.' How she got the words out, made this simulacrum of normal conversation when her head was reeling, was quite beyond her, but she did it somehow.

'You are very modest, *mademoiselle*.'

There was a tone in her voice that Alexa could not interpret. Her eyes went automatically to an exquisite seventeenth-century Claude beside the mantel, depicting a classical mythical episode in a vast landscape. 'It takes only a single great work, *madame*, to make anything else impossible,' she replied candidly.

Guy's mother inclined her head slowly. 'Yet modesty,'

she said, 'may go hand in hand with not inconsiderable natural gifts. The portrait you made of Guy confirms that to me. You have captured him well.' She paused, her eyes never leaving Alexa's.

Alexa swallowed, fighting for composure, remembering all that had come about because of that portrait. Remembering, with burning pain, how she had finally come to complete it, her heart torn to shreds by the man she was depicting. Then… 'Thank you,' she managed to get out, her eyes dropping to the floor. She could not look at Guy's mother.

'I wonder, *mademoiselle*, if you would consider painting me, as well as my son?'

Alexa's eyes few upwards. She swallowed again. Madame de Rochemont was regarding her, her gaze slightly questioning.

'I—I am sorry. No.' Alexa's reply seemed staccato, blunt, even to her own ears.

'No?' The arched eyebrows rose delicately. The questioning look was still in the eyes. More than questioning. That sense of being evaluated came over Alexa again. She felt her cheeks colour slightly. More than ever she wanted to get to her feet and walk out—as fast and as far as she could.

'I—I am sorry,' she said again.

There was a pause—the very slightest. 'Perhaps you would tell me why, *mademoiselle*.' It was politely said, but there was a hauteur in it that Alexa could hear clearly. She knew why—a *grande dame* such as Madame de Rochemont would not be used to hearing blunt refusals, especially to a commission that was intensely flattering, not to say valuable and prestigious.

Alexa pressed her lips together, trying to find an answer. 'I no longer practise portraiture, *madame*. I am so sorry.'

'I see. Would I be correct in thinking, therefore, that my son's portrait is the last you have made?'

Into Alexa's mind came the vivid, violent portrait that was the demonic twin of the one that had been a birthday gift for Guy's mother.

'My last professional portrait, yes,' she replied. 'It was a commercial commission. Done only for money.' Her voice was flat.

'Of course,' said Guy's mother. 'Why else would you wish to paint my son's likeness, *mademoiselle*?'

Alexa looked away. Back to the Claude beside the fireplace. She studied the figures, tiny against the broad pastoral expanse. One of the figures, at least, was blending into the landscape. It was Daphne, at the moment of her transforming into a laurel bush to escape the attentions of Apollo.

I escaped as well—becoming a recluse, hiding from life. Hiding from Guy. From what he wanted of me.

She looked away again, her gaze colliding with that of Guy's mother. The air froze in her lungs and dismay drowned her. Realisation dawned.

She knows. She knows what I was to her son...

Her face paled. Panic rose. Without conscious volition she got to her feet. She had to go now. Right now.

'I am sorry, Madame de Rochemont, but I must go.'

Guy's mother did not stand up. 'Before you do, I have a favour to ask of you.'

There was something different in her voice. Alexa didn't know what it was. Didn't know anything except that she had to go. Escape.

'I'm so sorry, but I really can't undertake the commission you mentioned—' she began, her voice hurried.

Madame de Rochemont held up a hand. A graceful, imperious gesture, cutting her off. 'That is not the favour,' she

said. Her voice was dry. Her expression was as unreadable
as ever, but there was a tension in it suddenly. She paused
a moment, then spoke. 'I would like you to go to France.
To talk to Guy.'

Alexa froze, disbelief in her eyes. Had she really heard
what she had? Had Guy's mother really said that? Why?
Why on earth…?

Words formed in her throat. Words that were impossible to say—impossible to get out—certainly not in front
of this formidable *grande dame* who was Guy's mother,
and who *knew* about Alexa and Guy. But she must say
something…

'That isn't possible.' Alexa's voice was flat. As flat as a
butterfly crushed by a rock.

'Why?'

Alexa's face closed. 'I think you will agree, *madame*,'
she said, with stony formality, 'that it would not be *comme
il faut.*'

The green eyes, so like the eyes she had once drowned
in, widened slightly.

'I do not understand you,' said Guy's mother.

Alexa pressed her lips, clenching her hands in her lap.
She looked directly at Madame de Rochemont. 'But your
daughter-in-law would, *madame*,' she said.

The older woman's face stilled.

'Ah,' she breathed slowly. Her eyes were fixed on Alexa.
She got to her feet. 'You must forgive me for insisting,' she
said, 'but it is imperative that you talk to Guy.'

'I have already said everything necessary.' Alexa's voice
was clipped. This was unreal—surreal. Standing here in
front of Guy's mother, who was telling her to talk to her
son.

About what, precisely? About how his marriage is

going? Is that it? What on earth is going on here? It doesn't make sense—any of it.

'But my son has not,' said Madame de Rochemont. 'And that is why you must go to France, to talk to him.'

Alexa stared, giving in. 'Look, what *is* going on?' she demanded, the edgy formality gone completely. 'I'm sorry if I sound impolite, but nothing here makes sense. Why am I here? What do you want of me, and why? I will be open with you—as I take it that you know that, much to my regret, my relationship with your son progressed beyond the professional one of client and artist. I had a brief affair with Guy last year—that's all. It meant…' She swallowed, but ploughed on. 'It meant as little to him as you might imagine. He informed me of his engagement, and terminated the relationship the same day. And, *madame*,' she emphasised, restraining herself from saying anything about Guy's subsequent attempt to restart it, 'the relationship remains terminated. If that is your concern, then you have my assurance that—'

Again, an imperious gesture with the hand silenced her. 'The only assurance I ask for is that you accede to my request to talk to my son.'

Alexa's chin went up. 'To what purpose?' she said bluntly. Her eyes met those of his mother—defiance in hers, his mother's unreadable.

'For the future happiness of my son,' said Madame de Rochemont.

Alexa's eyes closed. 'He may be as happy as he wishes, *madame*—it is nothing to do with me. I hope…' She took a breath, opening her eyes again to look straight at the woman who was asking something of her that was inexplicable and impossible to agree to. 'I hope he has a long and happy marriage.'

Something moved in the emerald eyes.

'So do I, Mademoiselle Harcourt. Any mother must wish that for their child. Which is why it is essential for you to talk to Guy.' She started to walk towards the door, and Alexa followed. 'It will take very little of your time,' said Guy's mother, talking over her shoulder. 'A car will take you to the airport, and you will be at the château in under two hours.'

'*Madame*, I cannot—'

Guy's mother stopped. Turned. 'Please,' she said.

What was it in her face, her eyes, that made Alexa stop as well? She bit her lip a moment, then simply nodded and said, 'All right. If you insist.' She gave a bewildered sigh, half throwing up her hand in concession. 'I don't understand why you are set on it—I cannot begin to imagine what you think it will achieve.'

'I think that Guy's wife,' said his mother, and her eyes met Alexa's full on, 'will find it the making of her marriage.'

So that was it. Now Alexa understood. She might have assumed the wrong Madame de Rochemont earlier, but it was indeed Madame Guy de Rochemont who needed assuring that Alexa did not pose a threat to her marriage. So, in order to allay her fears, the woman her husband had set up to provide an adulterous liaison had to be flown in, so that Guy could tell her to tell his wife—who had somehow found out about Alexa—that she was not, in fact, her husband's mistress.

She took a breath. 'I will do this, *madame*, but only on the condition that I will be free of further contact with any of your family. I want nothing more to do with any of you. I'm sorry if that sounds rude, but my life has moved on and that is that.'

The unreadable look was back in Madame de Rochemont's

eyes. 'As you wish, *mademoiselle*,' was all she said.
'Come—'

She led the way out of the room. Outside, one of her members of staff was waiting, and Guy's mother spoke to him in rapid French. Then she held out her hand to Alexa.

'Thank you.'

Reluctantly, Alexa shook the outstretched hand. '*Madame*,' she said formally. Then, clutching her bag more tightly than was necessary, she followed the member of staff back down the curving marble staircase. Her mind felt quite, quite numb.

CHAPTER NINE

ALEXA was still feeling numb as she took her seat on the private de Rochemont jet. It was familiar to her. She must have travelled on it half a dozen times, perhaps, during the months with Guy. The extravagance of it had shocked her, but he had been blunt about it.

'It saves time,' he had said to her.

And time was what he'd had least of. At any rate for her. So she had gone along with it, this outrageous extravagance, burning who knew how many carbon units, paying half a dozen salaries for the personnel required for a flight, simply to get herself, the woman Guy de Rochemont currently wanted to have sex with, to him at the time he wanted her.

I put up with it. I went along with it. I colluded with it.

Condemnation of her own behaviour bit at her.

I was as complicit as he was. Because I wanted to be. I wanted him on the terms he offered—because they were the only terms on offer. I told myself it was all right. It worked for both of us. That that justified it.

But it didn't.

I should have had the strength, then, to say no to those terms. To say no to him.

But she hadn't. She had gone along with it, made no demur, no question. Accepted it all.

Well, she had paid for it in the end, though. Paid for it even sooner than the end. Paid for it the moment she'd realised, with dawning dismay, that she had started to fall in love with Guy de Rochemont. And from that moment onwards he had held her to ransom. Held her heart to ransom. And her self-respect.

Well, she had her self-respect back again now. She had said no to being the mistress of an adulterous bridegroom, and she would make that clear to Guy's bride—as it seemed he now wanted her to do. Alexa should be glad that he cared, glad that he was finally showing consideration to the poor girl he'd married. Perhaps their marriage stood a chance now.

She must be glad of that.

What else could she be?

As the plane winged its brief way across the Channel, she made herself say that over and over. Ignoring the fingernails that were trying to scratch at her heart.

Let me get through this. Let me get through this and come away again. Back to the life I am going to lead now. The only life left to me.

A voice spoke at her side, making her turn her head.

'Miss Harcourt? The captain's compliments. We are starting our descent, and should be landing on schedule.'

The stewardess smiled politely at Alexa, and Alexa murmured something appropriate. Inside, her stomach started to knot. She took a breath, and then another. She could get through this. She *would* get through this. She must.

It was a mantra she repeated as the plane landed at a small private airfield west of Paris, and repeated again as she was escorted to a waiting limousine. It whisked her quickly and efficiently away, down a brief stretch of major roadway, to turn off after some miles onto a smaller country road. The weather was glorious, a perfect late afternoon in early summer, with the sun dipping low, turning the world to ripeness all around her. As the car slowed and turned down another narrow road, then drew up briefly to pass through ornate iron gates set in a two-metre high perimeter wall, she felt the knot tighten. She looked about her as the car moved along the smooth, long drive, curving through ornamental woodlands until it was clear of them to make visible a sight that made Alexa's breath catch.

Château Rochemont, a Loire château, was like something out of a fairy tale—palest grey stone and pointed towers, surrounded by vast, ornate parkland. As the car drew up at the front entrance and Alexa was ushered out, she glanced around as if she must surely see sauntering lords and ladies of the court, dressed for the very *fête* she had seen in the painting in Madame de Rochemont's London drawing room a bare two hours ago.

It's a different world—unutterably, incomparably different!

And it was the world Guy lived in. The one he'd visited her from, dipping into her modest bourgeois life to collect what he wanted from her, then leaving again to come back here. His home. Where he lived.

With his bride. His wife.

Her face closed. That was all she must remember—all that she must hold in her head. Nothing more than that.

She was ushered indoors—expected, that much was obvious. The huge entrance hall, with mirrors and gilt and chandeliers and a vast double staircase, took her breath away, but she showed no visible reaction. Her expression stayed closed. Composed.

Sang-froid—that was what she needed now. What she called upon.

Outwardly calm, she followed a member of staff along a wide *enfilade* stretching along to the right-hand side of the hall, then through into what seemed to be a separate wing. Her low heels tapped the parquet flooring and seemed to echo in the panelled corridor. Deliberately she did not look along the walls, though she was aware there were paintings everywhere, and niches holding statuary, which instinctively wanted to draw her eyes to them. But she steeled herself not to, steeled herself only to keep walking, ignoring the knotting in her stomach, until at length a pair of double doors was reached at the end of the corridor and the servant knocked discreetly at them.

A muffled, terse, *'Entrez—'* and the doors were opened for her. She walked in.

The room was double aspect, at the far end of the wing, and at first she saw only the huge sash windows in front of her and to her left-hand side. Then she saw a desk—huge, ornate.

Behind it sat Guy.

For a moment, just a moment, she saw his expression as it had been before her entry. Something like a blow struck her. There was such a bleakness in his face, such wintriness in his eyes! It was sudden pain, hurting her. Then, as he took in her presence in the doorway, his expression changed.

His face was transfixed. Completely immobile. As if a mask had dropped down over his features, shielding them from her. Then slowly, very slowly, he got to his feet. Distantly, Alexa heard the double doors behind her click shut.

'Alexa.'

Her name, nothing more. She had heard him say it in that bare, stark way before. But that time, at the cottage in Devon, it had been said differently. Emotion, dark and turbid, had been heavy in it. Now it was blank—completely blank.

She turned to face him fully. Face him, but not see him. She refused to see him. Refused to see his tall, lean figure, sheathed in a hand-made suit that fitted him as if it were moulded to his broad shoulders, his svelte hips. Refused to see the perfect planes of his face, the fall of his sable hair, the shape of his mouth, his jaw. The emerald, long-lashed eyes...

She refused to drown in them.

Her face was stony, as blank as his. Beneath the surface she could feel her stomach knot itself again, her lungs tighten. But she ignored it. It was imperative to ignore it.

'I was told you wanted to talk to me.'

Her voice was brusque.

His eyebrows drew across sharply. 'By whom?' he demanded. His voice seemed rough. She didn't care. Didn't care about its roughness. Didn't care about him. He was lost to her. For ever. And she did not care about that either. Must not care...

'By your mother,' she answered.

The mask vanished. Astonishment whipped across his face. 'My *mother*?'

'Yes, this afternoon. She invited me to visit her and told me you wanted to talk to me. She said it was important.' A heavy breath escaped her. 'So I have come.'

He seemed to be gathering his control.

'I find it...hard...to believe that,' he said slowly. His voice was harsh, grating at her. His eyes bored into hers, and she felt their force making her stance unsteady. 'When last I saw you, you made it very...clear...that you wanted nothing more to do with me.' He stood looking at her, his gaze like a knife to her flesh. 'I know what you think of me, Alexa. You made that unmistakable. Convincing.' His face tightened. 'Every line in that portrait on your easel told me that. Told me of your hatred for me.' His eyes darkened like a sunless forest. 'I should have told my mother about it. Then she would not have wasted her efforts getting you here.'

Alexa took a breath. Hard and heavy. Ignoring what she saw in him. Ignoring what it did to her.

'She said—' she took another breath '—it was important to your marriage. That's why I came—only for that reason.'

Guy stilled. 'My marriage…' He echoed the words. His brows snapped together disbelievingly. 'My mother talked to you about my marriage?'

She gave a rasp in her throat. 'It wasn't my idea—don't worry,' she said scathingly. 'She raised the subject. She said it was important I come here. Talk to you.' A heavy breath escaped her. 'So I have. I can only assume—' Her lips pressed tightly as she made herself say what she had to say. 'I can only assume that she means it's essential that your bride—' she said the word without the slightest trace of emotion, despite the knot in her stomach tightening like a ligature around a bleeding vein, oozing her lifeblood out of her body '—hears from me that I am no threat to her— that I never succumbed to your adulterous offer.'

'My bride.' His voice was flat. Stark. His eyes were veiled again, all emotion gone.

'Yes.' Alexa took another effortful breath. 'I don't know what chance of happiness she has, but what little I can give her I do. I wish her happiness—all that she can find.'

His eyes were on her. She could not read them. They were masked, opaque.

'That is…generous…of you,' he said slowly.

There was something different about him, but she could not tell what. She dared not look at him, dared not meet his gaze. But there was something different in his stance somehow, though he had not moved. He was immobile behind his desk, one manicured hand resting on its mahoghany surface. He was speaking again, and she made herself listen. Made her eyes meet his.

'Well, I can tell you,' he was saying, his eyes on hers, unreadable and veiled, but seeming all the same to be boring deep, deep into her, 'what I hope will reassure you, Alexa.' He paused, his eyes resting on hers like lead. 'Louisa is very happy in her marriage. Blissfully happy.'

Alexa swayed. Pain bit like a wolf, tearing at her throat. She made her mouth work. Forced it to work.

'I'm…glad. I'm very glad for her.'

'So am I,' said Guy. His eyes were still holding hers. 'She is deeply in love with her new husband.'

The wolf was tearing now, biting out her throat. 'I'm… I'm very glad for her,' she said again.

I must be glad. I must! She deserves that—every bride deserves that!

And every bride deserved a husband who loved her. Her expression changed, emotion rising in her throat, making her take a half-step towards him.

'Guy—' she spoke impulsively '—be…be kind to her! Don't do to her what you were planning on doing. Not with anyone. Please don't. If she's in love with you, don't hurt her—don't hurt her the way you hurt—'

She broke off. He was looking at her strangely, through that veiled mask.

'Did I, Alexa?' His words were slowly spoken. 'Did I hurt you?' There was something strained in his words. Did he feel bad that he had hurt her? she wondered.

She pressed her lips. Tried to look away, but could not. Yet she could not meet his eyes either. Then she spoke—admitting all, her voice drear, her words heavy.

'You didn't mean to, Guy. I know that. I know that the affair we had was…what it was. You were not responsible for my reaction to it. I chose to go along with it, with the affair, and the responsibility for my reaction is mine and mine alone. I should never, that night after the charity gala, have let you…let you…'

She swallowed, unable to finish. Then, with a shuddering breath, forced herself onwards. 'You have never been responsible for my feelings. And even if I deplored what you proposed—some adulterous, clandestine liaison— then that still does not make you responsible for what it did to me.' Her hands clenched at her sides. 'When you hunted me down, turned up at the cottage assuming I would come back to you simply because you wanted me to, I was glad you saw that second portrait. It spoke for me. Said everything!'

His eyes were pressing in on her, but they had changed. She could not tell how, or why, but they had all the same. She shut her eyes to shield herself from what was in his that she could not bear to see, then opened them again.

'What you wanted of me I no longer wished to give,' she said. Her words fell like stones. 'Even without the adulterous offer I would not have wanted it.' Her face worked. 'Flying here in your private jet reminded me all over again. How I'd been flown to you when you wanted me, and then flown home again. How you'd arrive when it suited you, and then leave again. I didn't want that.'

His expression tightened. 'You knew the limitations I was under from the start,' he said.

'I knew what they meant about what I'd thought I'd had with you.' She lifted her chin. 'It took me a long time, Guy, to face up to that. It wasn't until you made your…proposition…to me that I made myself see it. It showed me what I'd been to you all along—'

'What I'd been to you?' he echoed, cutting across her like a blade falling. He moved suddenly, abruptly, coming around the corner of the desk to face her.

He was too close, much too close, but she was too frozen to move.

'Do you know what you were to me, Alexa? Do you?' His voice was animated, urgent suddenly. 'You don't seem to know at all! I thought you did—but then—' his face twisted again '—I thought a lot I no longer think...' He spoke again, his eyes flashing now, green fire burning in his face. 'Look about you,' he ordered. His hand gestured, encompassing the high-tech equipment along one side of the room, the wide mahogany desk behind him, the lavish decor of the room, the vast domain of the château beyond the sweeping windows. 'What do you see?'

His eyes burnt greener. 'You see wealth, don't you? A château on the Loire. Stuffed with treasures. With art that could populate a museum. And this is only *one* of the de Rochemont properties! There are dozens of others— more!—all over the world. And you know what keeps them all? Keeps all the scores of de Rochemonts and Lorenzes living in the lap of luxury? Money—money that my family have been making for over two hundred years. Two centuries of accumulation, of wheeling and dealing and loaning and banking, to anyone and *everyone*. We're a byword for survival—we've survived *everything*! Because we guard everything we've got. No matter what history has thrown at us. Wars and revolutions and confiscations and proscriptions and competition and governments and commercial rivals. Every damn thing!'

He took a scissoring breath. 'But there's a price to be paid. Oh, it's a trivial one compared to the price that the mass of humanity has to pay for their survival, but it's a price all the same.' He looked at her, his expression bare.

'I pay in time, Alexa. *Time*. It's time that's my luxury—nothing else.' He glanced around at his palatial surroundings. 'Yes, mock if you will, but that is the truth to me. It is time that is my greatest treasure. And something more, as well.'

He took another breath. 'Do you know how many people there are in my life, Alexa? In my family?' He gave a short, abbreviated laugh. 'Too many. Too many. And they all want something of me. Namely: time. Business time and private time. I am deluged with relatives—deluged. And they all want my time. All of them.'

His expression changed again. 'Which is why my time with you—my brief, fleeting time with you—was so very precious.'

He shut his eyes a moment, then opened them again, and in them was something that made Alexa's breath catch.

'You were my haven, my respite. My repose. When I came to you, or you came to me, I could escape everything about my family, and just be with you. Only with you, Alexa. No demands on me. Only the two of us, together—the world shut away from us. All that I wanted. You with me. I thought…' His voice stumbled a fraction, then he went on. 'I thought it was what you wanted too. Just to be with me. It worked so well—so easily. It just seemed to happen. Without effort or difficulty. As natural as if it was ordained.

'Then I realised what you were—something I'd never found before in all my life. A woman who was not setting her cap at me, a woman who was actually indifferent to me, who didn't care whether I commissioned her or not, who paid me no attention other than to study me for her work, for whom I held no fascination other than deciding how to capture my likeness, who didn't even notice…' his voice became drier than ever '...that I desired her. And then—ah, then, Alexa—I knew what I wanted.' He paused.

'*You*. I wanted you. Just you. And you were everything that I wanted—in bed and out of it. In bed... Well, how could any man want more? Out of it... Ah, out of it you were peace and comfort, ease and quiet companionship. And I thought—'

There was a break in his voice now, an uncertainty that made Alexa's throat tighten. But not with the tearing of the wolf, with something quite different that she didn't dare think about. She dared not do anything other than stand and hear him speak to her.

'I thought that it was the same for you. That you understood what it was you gave to me that was so precious, and I hoped so much that I gave to you in return. That you understood why I wanted you—and that you understood...' his voice now had an edge in it, an edge that was a blade turned not against her but against himself '...why I had to end our relationship.'

He looked at her. 'I did not do that well, Alexa. I know that, and I am sorry for it. That morning when I severed you from my life, brutally and ruthlessly, because there was no other way I could bring myself to do it, it went against everything I wanted. I had to force myself to do it! Fighting every instinct that told me not to say those words to you! I had to force them out of me. The only way I could—'

She wrapped her arms around herself. It might help to stanch the wound. A wound he had reopened—a wound that had gouged so very deep in her, though she had tried so hard not to let him. Her eyes fell to the floor, picking out the lustrous blue and gold in the priceless carpet's pattern. Her breathing was shallow, difficult. Her expression anguished.

What was the point? What was the point in hearing this?

It was only torment—torment beyond any that she had thought possible—to hear him speak like this. And yet it was a treasure to her beyond imagining to know what she had once been to him.

But could never be again.

She lifted her head. Gazed right at him.

For a moment so brief, so precious, she felt emotion sweep through her—the emotion she had drained out of herself, forced out of herself, because there was no place for it, no point to it.

'You should have left it like that,' she said heavily. 'Let it go when you let me go.'

'I tried to. But I failed. I saw you again, saw you with another man, and I knew then that I could let no other man have you. I knew then that I could not let you go.' His eyes were holding hers again, as if it was essential to him, vital. 'I could not,' he said again.

'And I,' she answered, and her words were crystal clear, cost her what they would, 'could not comply with what you wanted. An adulterous affair. I never hated you till then. But then I did. It was all I felt for you.' She let the lie fall into the space between them, a space that could never now be bridged, that forever parted her from him.

For a long moment he just looked at her. Then, as if something had snapped inside him, he crossed to the window in front of his desk, looking out over the gardens of his château. There was tension across his shoulders. Abruptly, he turned, looking back at Alexa.

'Do you know,' he asked, and his tone was almost conversational, 'how many people work for Lorenz Investment? How many depositors it has? How many business loans? To how many firms? Employing how many people? Have you even *heard*,' he asked, 'of Lorenz Investment?'

'I take it,' Alexa replied, 'that is the bank owned by Louisa's father?'

'It is the bank,' Guy said, 'taken to the brink of *ruin* by Louisa's father. And because of that every single person employed at that bank, every firm that borrowed money, every organisation that lent it money, was at risk—of unemployment, of collapse, of ruin!' His face worked. 'Heinrich Lorenz, Louisa's father, had me at gunpoint. He knew that I would not, *could* not risk Lorenz Investment failing—or even merely to be at risk of failing—lest it start a fatal ricochet through all the other parts of Rochemont-Lorenz. He knew that the only way to allay suspicion was for me to have a convincing reason to invest in his bank.' He paused heavily. 'Like becoming his son-in-law.'

He looked across at Alexa, so far away now—so very far from this world in which vast amounts of money flowed, from this family that was a dynasty, a complex network of wealth and power.

'I didn't want to marry Louisa. But then...' his eyes shadowed '...I saw nothing strange about doing so. For two hundred years, Alexa, we have been making such marriages—both within the family and outside it. Louisa's parents made such a marriage, and she had been brought up to expect the same. My own parents had no particular desire to marry—but they did, and very successfully. When you are used to something like that it seems...normal. Unexceptional. Expected.'

He fell silent. All Alexa could hear was the subdued hum of the PC on Guy's desk. And the pulse of her heart. Telling her something she did not want to hear. Did not want to listen to.

Then, in a low voice, he spoke again. 'I went on thinking that—thinking that such a marriage was unexceptional, acceptable,' he said, 'right up until I had you in my arms again that night when I saw you at the charity gala. And I knew then, like lightning ripping through my being, that everything had changed! I wanted you, and I had to have you. I had to have you in my life. I could not do without you.' His jaw tightened. 'But I also could not let Lorenz Investment fail. Too much was at stake.'

She spoke.

'So you didn't. You didn't let it fail. I understand, Guy. Truly I do.' Her voice had hardened. 'I also understand why you thought you could have your bank-saving, emotionally empty dynastic marriage *and* have an adulterous liaison with me as well. I understand—but didn't condone. Never condone. And that is why—' she took another breath '—why I came here now. Simply to make it clear—as I know your mother must want me to, or else why should she have arranged all this?—to assure your bride of that.'

'Ah, yes, my bride.' There was no emotion in Guy's face.

'Yes. You said…' It was impossible to speak, but speak she must, with a strength she had to find. 'You said she was in love with you. That she was happy after all in her marriage. So if she needs to know about me—about what I am no longer to you—then I will tell her.' Resolution steeled her. Too much emotion was in her, but this had to be done. 'Where—where is she?'

There was a curious light in Guy's eyes. 'Louisa's on her honeymoon,' he said. For a moment time hung still, then Guy started to walk towards her. 'I told you—she's blissfully happy, in love with her husband. A husband,' he said, 'who doesn't happen to be me.'

CHAPTER TEN

ALEXA heard him say the words. Heard them clearly. But they made no sense.

Guy reached her. Lightly, very lightly, he cupped her elbows. Slowly her tightly crossed arms lowered, as if they had become too heavy—which was odd, because the room seemed to be swirling around her.

'I told you,' said Guy, 'that Louisa had agreed to marry me. Saw nothing to object to. But it seems—' his voice was dry '—someone else objected. Someone she'd known for a while. Someone who told her that a loveless dynastic marriage was anathema to the soul. Someone,' he finished, 'who persuaded her to marry him instead—because he was in love with her, and because she, after he'd pulled the scales from her eyes, was in love with him. So—' the green eyes glinted '—she jilted me and eloped.'

Too much was going through Alexa. It was as if electric currents were passing through her, overloading all her circuits.

'What about the bank? Lorenz Investment—?'

It was all she could think to say. All that was safe to say.

'Back from the brink,' said Guy. 'Just as I'd planned.'

She frowned, trying to make sense. 'But you had to marry Lousia—'

'No.' His eyes were holding hers. 'I had to let the world *think* I was marrying Louisa.' His expression changed. 'That was what I realised that night after the charity ball. When I knew that everything had changed. When I knew I had to have you back in my life. I could not marry Louisa.'

His hands cupping her elbows tightened. 'That was when I realised what I was going to have to do. Somehow I had to have it all—I had to protect the bank and have you, too. And I realised that I could do it if I could just keep the engagement going—because that would give me vital time, under cover of the betrothal, to pull together a rescue package. It was going to be a race, and it was going to be risky, but it could be done. I knew it could be done!'

Abruptly he loosed his grip, turning away from her, knuckling his fists on the mahogany surface of his desk. He twisted his head to look back at her.

'I thought myself so clever—thought I had found a way to make everything work out. Because I had to, Alexa.' His voice changed. 'The stakes had just become higher than I could bear to lose. That night—' his face worked '—that night when I made love to you again, I knew that I could *never* let you go! And I thought...' He paused, then went on, forcing himself to speak, 'I thought it was the same for you. That you would agree to what I was proposing. I was scared, Alexa—scared that it would be all too easy for you to take up with another man, like the damn man you'd been with that evening. So I had to keep you—any way I could!—while I sorted out the bank, got myself free of my engagement to Louisa.'

He went on raggedly. 'I was intending to tell you everything—talk to you—bare myself to you—make you understand the trap I was in. But you disappeared.'

He paused again, then made himself go on, his eyes

burning into hers. 'When I found you I discovered what a fool I'd been—an arrogant, conceited fool—to think you felt for me what I felt for you. And when I saw that portrait—' He broke off.

'Then I knew.' His voice was heavy, as heavy as a weight crushing him. 'I knew I was too late. I had made you hate me. And I had lost you.'

There was bleakness in his face—as bleak as the desert sands blown by witless winds.

The room, despite its cooling air-conditoining, was suddenly airless. Alexa's throat was blocked. She couldn't breathe.

'I—I need to get some fresh air,' she said faintly.

At once he was there, crossing to the pair of large French windows that opened on the other side of his desk out to the gardens. He threw them open and she hurried out, dragging in lungfuls of summer air. There was a little ornate garden bench, and gratefully she sank down on it. Her legs did not seem to be working.

Nor her mind.

Thoughts, emotions, swirled like a maelstrom, and she could make no sense of them—no form, no order. All the certainties she had lived with for so long now—certainties that had been like blades in her heart—had suddenly, in a few moments, dissolved to nothing...nothing at all. Desperately she tried to still the swirling maelstrom, make order of it, sense. She seized the one thought that swirled most vividly, most tormentingly. Seized it and stilled it and looked upon it.

Guy wasn't married. He hadn't married Louisa. He was never going to marry Louisa. And since the moment he had taken her to bed again he had never been going to marry Louisa.

The enormity of the realisation was like a tsunami going

over her. She seemed to sway as she sat, too weakened to move.

As arms came around her. Guy had lowered himself down beside her, his arm over her shoulder, steadying her.

'Alexa—'

There was anxiety in his voice. At least it sounded like anxiety—but what did she know? What did she know of Guy de Rochemont at all?

She twisted her head, looked at him.

'I don't know you,' she said.

His arm dropped from her, his expression transfixed.

'I don't know you,' she repeated. 'I've never known you.' She pulled a little away from him. 'But then...' Her throat tightened, and the words were so difficult to say, but she had to say them—she must look right into his face, his eyes, and say those words to him. 'I never tried to know you. Not in those months we were together—though the actual time we spent together was probably little more than a few weeks. But you had barriers all round you, keeping me out—keeping everyone out. I respected them, understood them, knew why you did it—because you were—are—a very private person. I am too. I...I keep myself to myself. Keep my emotions to myself. I'm...used to it. Just like you. That's why...at the time...I didn't mind the kind of relationship we had. It was only afterwards, when you came to me again, that I saw it differently. Made myself see it differently. As demeaning. Exploitative. With you just using me for convenient on-demand sex.'

She looked at him, looked into the troubled green eyes that held hers.

'But it wasn't. I had been right before. I'd understood what there was between us, and I should have trusted that. I should have trusted *you*. Instead—' her voice was heavy

'—I simply ran away, giving you no chance. No chance at all. No chance to talk to me, tell me what you intended.'

He disengaged his gaze from her, looking out over the gardens. The last of the sun caught the water in the stone-girded pond, which rippled lazily in a lift of air.

'But I never did talk to you, did I?' he said. 'Not about us. I just accepted what there was and was glad of it. Grateful for it. Grateful to have found a woman who could be, for me, an oasis in my life. So when I had to end it, had to agree to marry Louisa, all I could bear to do was—walk. Walk away. Leave that precious oasis you had become and instead walk out into a desert. Seeing you again...' He glanced at her now, a gaunt look on his face. 'It was like seeing a mirage, beckoning to me—promising me all that I could want. All that my life did not have any more. So I reached out, and I discovered—' his voice was strained '—I discovered it was, in truth, nothing more than a mirage. My own imagining. Not real at all.'

He leant forward, back hunched, forearms on his thighs, hands loose, staring at the water rippling in the stone basin, slowly draining of its light as the sun slipped away, off the gardens, behind the shadowing trees that marched along the borders.

She sat beside him a while, saying nothing. The maelstrom had gone now, sunk down through her, absorbed into her veins. Quieted. Somewhere she could hear birdsong.

She looked about her. It was so very beautiful, this spot, with the vista of the level gardens spreading all about her, the ancient mass of the château behind, and the lingering sunlight just catching the tops of the protecting trees. An oasis of beauty. Of quietness. And peace.

Peace of the heart.

Slowly, very slowly, in the warm, peaceful quietness, she reached for his hand, closing hers over his, winding her fingers into his. He pressed his into hers, holding her hand. Such a simple gesture. Saying nothing.

Saying everything.

He turned to her.

Tears were running down her face. Quietly, silently.

He gave a soft rasp in his throat. Then he put his arms about her, drawing her to him, holding her against him as they sat together, side by side. And still her tears came—so quietly, so silently.

Making words unnecessary.

Then he kissed away her tears and kissed her trembling mouth, kissed the hands he took again in his, raising them to his lips in homage, and she clung to his hand, and to him, and to his heart.

'*Ma belle* Alexa,' he murmured. Then he drew back a little. 'I thought you hated me,' he said wonderingly.

'So did I,' she said. 'But I was wrong.' She kissed his mouth. 'So wrong. It was still love…all along.'

'Still?' There was a questioning in his voice. Uncertainty.

'For so long. I don't know since when. Only that I fell in love with you knowing I should not—that it was…unwise beyond all things. A *folie d'amour*. There was no point in loving you—not even before I knew you were going to marry Louisa. Because what hope could there be in loving you—you who were who you were, from so different a world, wanting only what you did from me and for so brief a time? And when I knew about your betrothal, when you came back and I ran from you, refusing to listen to you, then there was no point in love at all. Only in hatred. And I poured it all—all my hatred—into that portrait of you. The one you saw.'

A voice from the French windows spoke. 'Just as you poured all your love into the one Guy gave me.'

Both started—Guy getting to his feet, drawing Alexa with him, her hands were still entwined in his.

'Maman—?'

Madame de Rochemont stepped out on to the gravelled terrace. How she had suddenly arrived, Alexa had no idea. But then, as a de Rochemont, what was there to stop her having a second private jet at her disposal?

'*Mon fils,*' she acknowledged. Then, coming up to Alexa, she kissed her on each cheek. 'Why do you think,' she asked her, 'I made sure I would know exactly the moment you returned to London?'

She took a step back, her regard encompassing them both.

'When it became clear to me that on no account should my son do what his father had done—what I had done— marry someone he did not love, I knew I must ensure it did not happen. Quite how to do it gracefully, I did not know. Sometimes, yes, such a marriage can be successful. But mine, Guy, was so because in the end I came to love your father, and he me. When I saw your portrait—the one you gave me—I knew.' Her voice changed. 'I knew you were already in love—and were loved in return.'

She met Alexa's eyes. 'That was why I told you I was grateful to have been given that portrait. Because it told me all that I needed to know.' She paused, her expression softening as she spoke to Alexa. 'I can tell who loves my son as much as I do. And I can tell—' she looked at Guy with the same look '—when my son is looking at someone with as much love as—from time to time!—he looks at me. And so,' she went on, 'there was only one last mystery to solve. Why the two of you were not together. A mystery,' she finished, with the air of one delivering a *coup de théâtre*, 'solved not three hours ago, when you, *ma chère*, recommended I consult my daughter- in-law on the action

I was—in desperation to resolve this *impasse*—urging you to take.'

She glared at Guy. 'How could you not have told her Louisa had eloped, and solved your problem *tout court*?'

'Maman,' he answered, tight-lipped, 'it was not that simple—'

Madame de Rochemont gave another imperious wave of her hand. 'Love is always simple. It is men who are fools to think it is not! Do you not agree, *ma chère* Alexa?'

'I think, *madame*, it is also women who can be fools—as I was.'

'Well, I am sure Guy gave you cause. But now I can see that finally all is resolved, and that is a great relief to me. Ah…' her voice lifted '…perfect timing.'

Guy and Alexa turned to see what the cause was. Guy's face blanched, and Alexa could only stare, eyes widening.

Along the façade of the château a grand procession was approaching, its lead a resplendent personage in a velvet jacket, bearing a vast silver salver held in front of him with both hands. On it nestled a champagne bottle in an ice bucket, next to three flutes, and behind him three equally resplendent but lesser personages bore aloft silver salvers groaning with dishes of canapés and *hors d'oeuvres*. They were followed by a dozen uniformed staff carrying between them a gilded antique table and three matching chairs, which they proceeded to set down, with great precision, on the terrace. Upon the table with a practised flourish, the salvers were placed, one after another, and then the champagne bottle was opened and the flutes filled to perfection.

All the attendant staff stood back, apparently staring fixedly ahead, as well-trained staff would always do, but Guy knew they were actually riveted with full and absolute attention on Alexa. They clearly realized—given the dramatic circumstances not only of her sudden unscheduled arrival, but also the arrival of his mother, not to mention the fact that he was still clasping her hand—that she was, *evidemment*, to be their new *châtelaine*.

With admirable composure Guy thanked them, his expression a picture, and they withdrew in good order.

'I'm sorry,' he apologised to Alexa. Embarrassment was clear in his face at all this over-the-top grandeur.

'Quite unnecessary,' said his mother airily. 'Alexa is perfectly familiar with the concept of a *fête champêtre*. We have already discussed my predilection for the art of the Rococo—and I confess I am much looking forward to showing her all the paintings hanging here, too. It is always enjoyable to discuss these matters with professional artists. Their eye is quite different from that of a mere amateur such as myself. But that is for later—we have many years ahead, my dear, for you to give me your opinions, and of course to choose your own additions to the collection. Guy is far too much of a barbarian for it to be necessary to regard *his* tastes, so I never do,' she finished dismissively, and she led the way forward to the table.

'Come!' She lifted her hand to them, seating herself regally at the foot. Guy pulled out the chair beside him for Alexa, and sat himself down at the head of the table. He handed a glass of champagne to his mother, and another to Alexa.

She was in a daze—a daze of incredulous happiness— happiness so full, so complete, that it was carrying her on an iridescent rainbow to heaven. She tried to think, to understand—but it was impossible. Impossible to do anything other than what she was doing: letting Guy take her hand once more and hold it loosely, possessively, across the table, as they raised their glasses at his mother's instigation.

'To you both,' said Madame de Rochemont, her eyes suddenly soft, and full with emotion. 'To your love. And to your long and happy marriage.'

Together, Guy and Alexa tilted their flutes to drink, and the setting sun turned the champagne to molten gold. As golden as their happiness, and their future yet to come.

EPILOGUE

'DON'T move. Stay just like that—'

Guy stilled, lounging back against the sun-warmed rock behind him. The instruction to stay still was not a problem. Nothing in the world was a problem any more. He relaxed gazing out over the incredible Alpine panorama of soaring mountains. Some rocky peaks were still topped with pristine snow, even now in the high summer, and the lower slopes were garbed in verdant green, plunging down to deep valleys far below. Here on the upper slopes, where they had walked on this wonderful sunlit day, the air was like breathing crystal—clear and sharp. Making him feel so alive...

His gaze went out over the soaring vista, focussing on the eagle rising lazily on the thermals. As free as the wind that bore it upwards. As free as he now was. Free to live the life he wanted—and, oh, more than that! The life that he hadn't even dreamt could ever be his. The life that was like a precious, precious jewel—and that jewel was here, so close he could reach out his hand and stroke the tender curve of her calf. Her legs were half drawn under her as she rested the sketchpad on her knees, her wide brow furrowed in concentration as her pencil worked across the paper. He gazed lovingly at her as she worked.

Alexa—his Alexa! His beautiful, beloved Alexa! He felt

his heart fill with emotion, with love. Oh, she was a jewel indeed. He had thought her lost—thought he had driven her away—but she had come back to him, given him the gift of her heart, her love. And he would treasure it all his life. His eyes softened. For a moment he saw her as he had first seen her—lifting her gaze to his and doing exactly what she was doing now: reeling! He had seen it then, at their very first meeting, and it had sent a shot of lightning through him, a satisfaction so intense he had known even in that moment that getting this beautiful, wonderful woman to gaze at him with the same rapt expression was worth everything in the world to him.

For a moment that raptness held, and then he saw her expression change—liquefy and transmute—into something so much more than what it had first been. Now, as his gaze mingled with hers, and hers softened to his, between them flowed the message of their love—strong and pure and eternal.

Then her expression changed yet again, and her mouth pursed.

'Stop it—I can't concentrate,' she admonished sternly.

A smile played at his mouth. 'Of course you can,' he replied. He stretched back, lengthening his legs and crooking his arms behind his head, lean and relaxed. 'You just concentrate on me, *ma belle*.'

His evident satisfaction at this state of affairs drew an answering smile. Alexa put aside her sketchpad.

'It's hopeless,' she said. 'I want to draw you, but I can't. You are far, far too distracting. I don't want to draw you—I want to kiss you.'

She leant forward, her hand cupping the outline of his jaw, and brushed his mouth with hers.

He folded her to him, nestling her against his heart as they both gazed out over the breathtaking vista all about them.

'It was so good of Louisa and her gorgeous young bridegroom to lend us their chalet for our honeymoon,' she said.

A frown creased Guy's brow. 'Gorgeous?' he growled, in mock anger.

She glinted up at him. 'Well, he *is* gorgeous—if you like those sort of looks. Which Louisa obviously does. Even though I—' she gave a mock sigh '—am utterly addicted to green eyes, and so sadly young Stefan leaves me quite unmoved.'

'That's better,' said Guy, and hugged her more closely against him. 'I'm glad you like Louisa, though—she's a nice kid.'

'Pretty, too—much prettier now she isn't being forced to wear those formal clothes her mother chose for her,' said Alexa.

She'd met Louisa properly now, when Alexa and Guy had arrived from their lavish wedding reception at the château the day before and the young couple had shown the honeymooners around their chalet before heading off down the mountain themselves, to visit Stefan's family on the far side of the range. Louisa had been first astonished, then delighted, and then smug when she'd recognised Alexa from their initial anonymous meeting in the hotel powder room.

'Didn't I tell you that you were exactly the sort of woman Guy would go for? Elegant and *soignée*—unlike me!' She'd grinned. 'And that ring looks far, far better on you than it ever could on me.'

Alexa had glanced down at the huge betrothal ring glittering on her finger. 'I'm afraid I've done what I advised *you* to do—asked for another one for everyday wear. I'm keeping this for best!'

Now, as she sat within the circle of Guy's arms, high on

the alpine slope, only the simple gold band of her wedding ring adorned her hand. She glanced at it wonderingly.

'Are we really married?' she asked dazedly.

Guy smiled, humour tugging at his mouth. 'How could you doubt it? Did our wedding not have sufficient impact on you? A packed cathedral, a wedding breakfast that could have graced a Renaissance feast, and enough champagne to float a battleship! I lost count of how many hundred guests there were. And even I do not know just how many relatives I have. Even more than those who decided they could not bear to miss seeing you make me the happiest of men!'

He moved her more comfortably into the circle of his arms and she nestled close against him. More happiness than she could bear filled her.

'Will your family forgive you for marrying an outsider?' she asked.

Guy shrugged a shoulder. 'It's of no importance to me,' he said, 'and besides...' wry humour tugged at his mouth again '...one good thing about marrying you is that it means I am not favouring one branch of the family over another. But if we are talking of forgiveness,' he went on, and his voice was serious now, 'although she was very civil to me as your bridesmaid, will your friend Imogen forgive me for my treatment of you? When I was desperately trying to find you after you'd run from London, and I contacted her to see if she knew where you were, she was not...well-disposed...towards me.'

'I think,' said Alexa mischievously, 'that you have now convinced her of your honourable intentions! Besides, she is deliriously in love herself now, and that makes her charitable.'

Guy laughed. 'Ah, yes—that man I thought might threaten my claim on you. It was actually Imogen who interested him! How blind can the man be?' he said, his prejudice blatant.

'Richard agreed to ask me out as a kindness, because Imogen was so keen to take my mind off you—but, so she's told me now, it was *her* he was hoping to impress. And eventually she got the message.'

'These obdurate women, *hein*!' he exclaimed humourously. 'So, *dis-moi*...' He smoothed the pale fall of her hair from her shoulder. 'Are you truly happy to spend your honeymoon on a mountain miles from everywhere? In a humble mountain chalet?'

'Completely,' Alexa assured him. 'I like living in the back of beyond—I've done it in Devon, and I've done it in a desert. An alpine mountain is a welcome addition to my list. But are *you* sure,' she asked, and the mischievous note was back in her voice, 'that you can acclimatise to this after all the splendours of your natural environment.' She waved an arm around the airy vista.

'I revel in it,' Guy assured her. His eyes softened. 'Don't you yet believe how much I crave the quiet life—not the three-ring five-star circus I usually have around me?' His expression changed again—a more serious note entered his voice. 'Now that Heinrich's bank is safe—and so, thank goodness, are all the other parts of Rochemont-Lorenz— I'm going to ease off. Running everything hands-on brought my father to an early grave, I'm sure of it, and I won't go that way, Alexa.' His voice was resolute. 'Our wealth is quite enough,' he went on dryly, 'and I'm going to set up a more federated management structure—spread the load more. The bank nearly cost me the most precious treasure of all—you.' He tilted his head, cupping her cheek in his hand. 'I could not live without you, Alexa *ma belle, mon coeur*—not for a day—not for a lifetime.'

He kissed her tenderly, and she kissed him back. Then

they both relaxed back against the rock. All around was silence, with only the occasional tinkling of a cowbell from far away, or the wind soughing in the bare rocks of the peak towering above them.

'It's a good mountain,' said Guy approvingly.

'Better than a global historic banking house?' Alexa queried wryly.

'If I had to choose, then, in the end, yes. I am proud of my heritage, I will not deny that, but mountains last a lot longer than banks. I think Stefan is richer than I in that respect.'

'They'll be happy, won't they, the two of them—Louisa and Stefan—turning this place into a nature reserve?' said Alexa.

'Blissfully,' Guy assured her.

'Will Louisa's parents forgive her, do you think? Jilting you to run off with Stefan?'

'Oh, yes,' Guy said dryly. 'Annelise and Heinrich are two of the biggest snobs I know, and they've got far, far more than they deserve. Louisa told me they went ballistic at first, hearing she'd run off with some drop-out green crusader she'd met through those friends in London she'd been staying with. They saw all their hopes of having a grandchild of theirs running the whole of Rochemont-Lorenz evaporating before their ambitious eyes. But then—' his eyes glinted mordantly '—they realised that I'd bailed out Heinrich's wretched bank for them anyway. And then they realised that they'd snaffled a much, much bigger prize for their wayward daughter. One to set their snobbish hearts aglow. I would have just *loved* to have seen Louisa introduce him when she finally dragged him to that ducal *schloss* of theirs!'

'Prince Stefan of Andovaria,' supplied Alexa, her eyes laughing.

'Yes, indeed. Only a younger son, but it's the title that counts,' said Guy sardonically. 'And now Stefan can be as green as he likes, with their blessing, and live in any eco-chalet he wants—for he owns his own mountain and his cousin is a sovereign prince, so their daughter takes social precedence over every person in *this* family! Heinrich and Annelise are very pleased with Louisa.'

'I'm glad,' said Alexa. 'And I'm glad, and so relieved, that your mother, Guy, doesn't mind my marrying you.'

'She approves of you enormously.' His voice was wry again. 'And not just because you have made me the happiest of men. You are unimpressed by all our wealth—but *very* impressed with our art collection. And best of all—' he kissed her affectionately on her nose '—you are polite about her saccharine Rococo paintings!'

'Well, they have their charms,' allowed Louisa.

His mouth curved. 'And so do you, Madame Guy de Rochemont.' A new note entered his voice, doing what it always did to her, what she knew it would always do, all her days—weakening her limbs like honey. 'Charms so plentiful, so alluring, so…enticing…that there is only one thing to be done…'

The jewelled green eyes poured into hers, reaching her soul. Her heart.

'This…' said Guy.

His mouth was soft as velvet. His touch as fine as silk.

His love as long as life.

And so was hers for him.

Coming Next Month

from **Harlequin Presents® EXTRA.** Available December 7, 2010.

Coming Next Month

from **Harlequin Presents®.** Available December 28, 2010.

REQUEST YOUR FREE BOOKS!

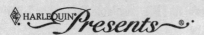 HARLEQUIN *Presents*

2 FREE NOVELS PLUS
2 FREE GIFTS!

YES! Please send me 2 FREE Harlequin Presents® novels and my 2 FREE gifts (gifts are worth about $10). After receiving them, if I don't wish to receive any more books, I can return the shipping statement marked "cancel." If I don't cancel, I will receive 6 brand-new novels every month and be billed just $4.05 per book in the U.S. or $4.74 per book in Canada. That's a saving of at least 15% off the cover price! It's quite a bargain! Shipping and handling is just 50¢ per book.* I understand that accepting the 2 free books and gifts places me under no obligation to buy anything. I can always return a shipment and cancel at any time. Even if I never buy another book, the two free books and gifts are mine to keep forever.

106/306 HDN E5M4

Name   (PLEASE PRINT)

Address   Apt. #

City   State/Prov.   Zip/Postal Code

Signature (if under 18, a parent or guardian must sign)

Mail to the **Harlequin Reader Service:**
IN U.S.A.: P.O. Box 1867, Buffalo, NY 14240-1867
IN CANADA: P.O. Box 609, Fort Erie, Ontario L2A 5X3

Not valid for current subscribers to Harlequin Presents books.

Are you a current subscriber to Harlequin Presents books and want to receive the larger-print edition? Call 1-800-873-8635 today!

* Terms and prices subject to change without notice. Prices do not include applicable taxes. N.Y. residents add applicable sales tax. Canadian residents will be charged applicable provincial taxes and GST. Offer not valid in Quebec. This offer is limited to one order per household. All orders subject to approval. Credit or debit balances in a customer's account(s) may be offset by any other outstanding balance owed by or to the customer. Please allow 4 to 6 weeks for delivery. Offer available while quantities last.

Your Privacy: Harlequin Books is committed to protecting your privacy. Our Privacy Policy is available online at www.eHarlequin.com or upon request from the Reader Service. From time to time we make our lists of customers available to reputable third parties who may have a product or service of interest to you. If you would prefer we not share your name and address, please check here. ☐

Help us get it right—We strive for accurate, respectful and relevant communications. To clarify or modify your communication preferences, visit us at www.ReaderService.com/consumerschoice.

HP10R

HARLEQUIN®

A *Romance*

FOR EVERY MOOD™

Spotlight on

Classic

Quintessential, modern love stories
that are romance at its finest.

See the next page
to enjoy a sneak peek from
the Harlequin Presents® series.

Harlequin Presents® *is thrilled*
to introduce the first installment of
an epic tale of passion and drama by
USA TODAY *Bestselling Author*
Penny Jordan!

When buttoned-up Giselle first meets
the devastatingly handsome Saul Parenti,
the heat between them is explosive....

"LET ME GET THIS STRAIGHT. Are you actually suggesting that I would stoop to that kind of game playing?"

Saul came out from behind his desk and walked toward her. Giselle could smell his hot male scent and it was making her dizzy, igniting a low, dull, pulsing ache that was taking over her whole body.

Giselle defended her suspicions. "You don't want me here."

"No," Saul agreed, "I don't."

And then he did what he had sworn he would not do, cursing himself beneath his breath as he reached for her, pulling her fiercely into his arms and kissing her with all the pent-up fury she had aroused in him from the moment he had first seen her.

Giselle certainly *wanted* to resist him. But the hand she raised to push him away developed a will of its own and was sliding along his bare arm beneath the sleeve of his shirt, and the body that should have been arching away from him was instead melting into him.

Beneath the pressure of his kiss he could feel and taste her gasp of undeniable response to him. He wanted to devour her, take her and drive them both until they were equally satiated—even whilst the anger within him that she should make him feel that way roared and burned its resentment of his need.

She was helpless, Giselle recognized, totally unable to withstand the storm lashing at her, able only to cling to the man who was the cause of it and pray that she would survive.

Somewhere else in the building a door banged. The sound exploded into the sensual tension that had enclosed them, driving them apart. Saul's chest was rising and falling as he fought for control; Giselle's whole body was trembling.

Without a word she turned and ran.

Find out what happens when Saul and Giselle succumb to their irresistible desire in

THE RELUCTANT SURRENDER

Available January 2011 from Harlequin Presents®

MARGARET WAY

Wealthy Australian,
Secret Son

Rohan was Charlotte's shining white knight
until he disappeared—before she had
the chance to tell him she was pregnant.

But when Rohan returns years later as
a self-made millionaire, could the blond,
blue-eyed little boy and Charlotte's heart
keep him from leaving again?

Available January 2011